Angels, Arguments and a Furry Merry Christmas

Colin and I jerked to attention at the sound of three voices in unison roaring "*Rolf!*", before a thunder of paws sent Colin leaping through the bannister on to me as our dopey dog tore past him on the stairs.

"What happened?" I asked, bursting back into the living room and trying to prise Colin's petrified claws out of my chest as he clung on for dear life. (I appreciated the fact that he'd immediately turned to me for comfort, but puncture wounds in the skin are *so* not a good look.)

Nobody answered me, but I just had to check out their faces to see that something was badly wrong. And then I spotted her; or what was left of her. Rolf had chewed up our angel – then spat out lumps of her when he realized she wasn't made out of marzipan or bread or dog food or anything else digestible.

Now we had no tree, no decorations, and no Mum-made angel.

Merry Christmas, Rolf, and thanks a lot…

Available in this series:

The Past, the Present and the Loud, Loud Girl
Dates, Double Dates and Big, Big Trouble
Butterflies, Bullies and Bad, Bad Habits
Friends, Freak-Outs and Very Secret Secrets
Boys, Brothers and Jelly-Belly Dancing
Sisters, Super-Creeps and Slushy, Gushy Love Songs
Parties, Predicaments and Undercover Pets
Tattoos, Telltales and Terrible, Terrible Twins
Mates, Mysteries and Pretty Weird Weirdness
Daisy, Dad and the Huge, Small Surprise
Rainbows, Rowan and True, True Romance(?)
Visitors, Vanishings and Va-Va-Va Voom
Crushes, Cliques and the Cool School Trip
Hassles, Heart-Pings! and Sad, Happy Endings...
Angels, Arguments and a Furry Merry Christmas
A Guided Tour of Ally's World

And coming soon, a whole new world...
Stella Etc.:
Frankie, Peaches & Me
Sweet-Talking TJ
Meet the Real World, Rachel

Find out more at
www.karenmccombie.com

ALLY'S WORLD

ANGELS, ARGUMENTS AND A FURRY MERRY CHRISTMAS

KAREN McCOMBIE

SCHOLASTIC

for all the angels, shepherds and wise men
(and everyone else!) at west green school.

Scholastic Children's Books,
Commonwealth House, 1–19 New Oxford Street,
London WC1A 1NU, UK
A division of Scholastic Ltd
London ~ New York ~ Toronto ~ Sydney ~ Auckland
Mexico City ~ New Delhi ~ Hong Kong

First published in the UK by Scholastic Ltd, 2002
This edition published by Scholastic Ltd, 2004

Copyright © Karen McCombie, 2002
Cover illustration copyright © Spike Gerrell, 2002

ISBN 0 439 95945 4

Printed and bound by AIT Norhaven A/S, Denmark

10 9 8 7 6 5 4 3

Contents

PROLOGUE   1

1:   'TIS THE SEASON TO BE SMASHING...   3

2:   SNOW BALLS? (S)NO(W) THANKS...   14

3:   THE JOYS OF FESTIVE FIGHTING   20

4:   A NIGHT WITH RACHEL'S TROUSERS...   29

5:   WEIRD DREAMS AND DAFT DOGS   36

6:   FIRST TIME, FAST TIME   42

7:   NOT FAIRY NICE   47

8:   ANOTHER FRIEND, ANOTHER HUFF   55

9:   AND THE WINNER IS ... A SHOCK   60

10: WALKING IN A LOO-ROLL WONDERLAND...   65

11: OOF! WHEE! AND BLEE!   72

12: DULL DATES AND SACKED SISTERS   79

13: JINGLE BALLS   85

14: LINN'S "LOVELY" SURPRISE   90

15: BAD BREATH, BAD JOKES   94

16: THE UNDRESSED REHEARSAL   98

17: THE DIFFERENCE BETWEEN "OOH" AND "AHH"   104

18: THE BRANCH IN THE BASEBALL CAP 109

19: MISSING: ONE DUMB DOG 118

20: LAYING (VERY) LOW... 122

21: YET ANOTHER "SECRET" FRIEND 128

22: SHEEP, HAMSTERS AND THE LITTLE BABY JESUS 132

23: POTATOES TO THE RESCUE! 137

24: NOT SO ANGELIC... 141

25: CHLOE AND THE NON-STOP HAIR-TOSSING 146

26: EMERGENCY! ANGEL NEEDED *NOW!* 150

27: SANTA GETS IT *SO* WRONG 155

28: ICE-COLD ICE AND HOT RIBENA... 159

29: SING-A-LONG-A-CHRISTMAS-CAROL 163

30: INVASION OF THE SNOW ANGELS... 168

PROLOGUE

Dear Mum,

It's the summer holidays – hurrah! And I'm bored out of my head – boo!

It's not fair, is it? I have this great hunk of free time and absolutely no one to spend it with. OK, so I'm exaggerating slightly ("No!" – a shocked nation). Dad, Linn and Rowan are all busy working, Tor is off doing some summer school craft workshop thing, and practically all my mates' families have spookily chosen this week to go on holiday. Which leaves two people for me to hang around with: Grandma and Kyra.

Now you may think I'm insane to pass up the chance of non-stop merriment, but I just *had* to turn down Grandma's offer to help her spring clean (summer clean?) every cupboard in our house. And Kyra; well, Kyra is always pretty entertaining, but she likes to verge on the *annoying* side too, so you have to limit your time with her in order to stay sane.

So, to cut a long, rambling story slightly shorter, I'm going to while the week away by doodling down what happened to us all last Christmas, i.e. the Christmas *before* I started writing all the journal-type things for you earlier this year. In other words, this is Christmas BK –

Before Kyra. In fact, before *lots* of people and stuff I've told you about by now: before Stanley (the man *and* the goldfish); before Britney (the pigeon, *not* the pop diva); before Michael and Harry (our new, improved neighbours*); before Dad disgraced himself and took up line-dancing (how could he scar his own children this way?).

So, I guess you could call this a "prequel". Hey, if it's good enough for *Star Wars*, it's good enough for me...

Love you lots,

Ally

(your Love Child No. 3)

(*They are a great improvement on grouchy old Mr and Mrs Fitzpatrick, our former neighbours, who I'm sure you will remember with no fondness at all. But then again, having a tyrannosaurus rex with a collection of venomous and bad-tempered pet stingrays move in would be an improvement on Mr and Mrs Fitzpatrick...)

Chapter 1

'TIS THE SEASON TO BE SMASHING...

Lots of people have traditions leading up to Christmas, like opening advent calendars, or playing bad Christmas compilation CDs till everyone's sick of the theme from *The Snowman*, or sneaking a look at the presents under the tree and then taping them back up and hoping no one notices.

I guess we're just a normal(ish) family, with normal traditions. One of ours happens to be fighting over the arrival of a certain Christmas card every year...

"Linn, you *didn't*!" I gasped, staring at the card and the accompanying gruesome photo on the mantelpiece.

"I did," said Linn, matter-of-factly, as she pointed the remote at the TV and tried to flick between the Saturday morning shows. (I say *tried*; she didn't know that the remote wasn't working 'cause I'd nicked the batteries out of it last night for Tor's glow-in-the-dark bat clock.)

"But, Linn, how *could* you?"

"Because I *wanted* to and because I couldn't wait for you lazy lumps to get out of bed before I opened it."

You know, my oldest sister Linn might be many things (grumpy, bossy, irritatingly pretty, unnaturally tidy), but there's one thing you can always be sure of with her; she's *always* honest. That's honest in a *bad* way, as well as a *good* way. By bad, I mean she'll tell you straight if she hates your new clothes, or that your latest hairstyle makes you look like a horse in a wig, or that your cooking skills are so awful that it's probably best to call the ambulance before anyone starts eating, just to save time. (I'd give you examples of her being honest in a good way, but I can't actually think of any just this second.)

So, I guess she was only being honest when she explained tearing open Uncle Joe's card by saying it was because she "wanted to". But how could she live with herself, breaking with family tradition like that? Whenever our once-a-year communication arrives from our Canadian relatives, me, Linn, Rowan and Tor all gather together around the exotically stamped envelope and *then* fight to the death over who gets to open it first. (Chosen method last year: a game of Scissors, Paper, Stone.)

Whoever's won then discards the envelope and corny card (with its predictably short and unimaginative "Merry Christmas from Joe, Pauline and the twins!" message) and we all cram around, ready to ooh and aah at this year's photo of our twin elves. Sorry – twin cousins.

"I've been awake for hours – what do you expect? You'd have done the same." That's how Linn expanded on her excuse as I went over to examine this year's photo and shudder at the sight of Carli and Charlie.

"They don't get any prettier, do they?" I commented, lost in awe at our cousins' sour, pointy little faces.

I know that sounds mean, but it's not just the fact that these kids are funny-looking. Funny-looking can be fine; funny-looking can be quite cute in a kid. It's more that our cousins have had the same vaguely evil expressions on their identical funny-looking faces ever since they were babies. Put it this way, if they'd been brought up in New Zealand instead of Canada, they'd have been snapped up straight away as extras in any evil troll scenes when they were filming *Lord of the Rings*.

"Awww! You opened the card from Uncle *Joe*!" came the voice of a small, indignant Spiderman (with his trusty soft-toy penguin tucked under his arm), from the living-room doorway.

"Well, you should have woken up at a decent hour and maybe I would've been able to resist temptation!" Linn grinned at our little brother Tor, who came padding over to my side to study this year's snapshot.

"Yeuchh!" he squealed in distaste, as Carli and Charlie gave him the evil eye.

"So how come you slept in, Tor?" I asked, surprised at the notion of our mini Dr Dolittle neglecting his morning duty as breakfast waiter for our many and varied pets.

"Ticking," he shrugged.

Ah ... ticking. Now what could our boy-of-very-few-words mean by that?

"Your clock was ticking?" Linn hazarded a guess.

"Uh-huh," Tor nodded, holding the snap of Carli and Charlie up high, now that Rolf had wandered over and started licking it on the off-chance that it was made of edible photographic paper. "Too loud."

"What – your clock was ticking so loud it kept you awake?" I checked with him.

I got another nod for that. Oh, well – at least that

meant I could put the batteries back in the TV remote (when Linn wasn't looking).

"Merry Christmas, everybody!"

Me, Linn, Tor and Rolf jumped in surprise. The first surprise was that Rowan was actually awake on a Saturday morning before midday, and the second was that she was wishing us a Merry Christmas just a *few* days earlier than we might have expected. Twenty-five days too early to be exact.

"Decorations!" Tor cried gleefully, and ran towards Rowan and the battered cardboard box she was carrying in her arms.

"Yeah, I just woke up and thought: it's the first of December. Yay! It's practically Christmas! So I dragged this out of the attic cupboard – we can do up the house this morning to get us in the festive mood!"

"Brilliant idea!" said Linn sarkily, from the comfort of the saggy armchair. "Then maybe this afternoon we can roll our Easter eggs!"

Rowan pursed her lips but otherwise ignored Linn, which is often the best thing to do to prevent a full-scale bickerthon breaking out between those two. Instead she began lowering herself and the box down gracefully to the floor like a Japanese geisha. And she did look very like a geisha today, in her ancient patterned silk kimono. And like a geisha, she was wearing a lot of make-up; although *unlike* a geisha, it hadn't been immaculately applied this morning – it was just the smeared leftovers of the party make-up she hadn't bothered washing off last night before bed. (By the looks of her panda eyes, there was going to be some *serious* mascara streaks on her white pillow. Grandma was going to be *mighty* happy about that next laundry day.)

Course, elegant geisha girls teeter along in those high-rise shoes that are a cross between a block of wood and a flip-flop. They don't tend to wear slippers in the shape of pink furry pigs, at least not in the photos *I've* ever seen of them. I think Rowan was regretting wearing her new slippers right at that second, since Rolf was taking a particular liking to them and trying to wrestle them off her feet.

"Rolf, leave!" I told him sternly, just as his chewing made Rowan wobble on the last couple of centimetres of her descent and she ended up crashing both her knees and the box on to the floor.

Rolf stopped, momentarily alarmed by the smashing, tinkling noise that had just come from the box – and then went back to chewing the heel of Rowan's slipper.

"Nice one, Rolf..." Linn rolled her eyes.

Without a word, Dr Dolittle/Spiderman stepped in, taking Rolf by his worn leather collar and gently dragging him away out into the hall.

"Here," I said to Rowan, passing her a paper hankie to wipe the drool off her heel.

"Thanks. Well, bang goes one of the tree decorations! Just as well tinsel can't break..."

My sister's eyes were shining, as Rowan's always do when there's anything glittery and sparkly to look at. It's funny, you know, but it always *is* kind of exciting to pull all the decorations out of their box and gawp at the familiar twinkly bits. All the tree decorations in particular we loved – they were very, *very* old-fashioned, handmade, hand-painted glass baubles that our Grandma Love used to have, before she passed them on to our parents when *they* were poor and *she* fancied treating herself to some nice new ones out of Woollies.

"Oh…" mumbled Rowan, opening the lid and staring at the damage. After a moment's scrutiny, she delicately put her hands inside and pulled out two metal hooks with coloured shards of glass dangling from them where pretty baubles used to be. Not so much festive as *lethal*, if you ask me.

"Are they *all* like that?" I gulped, as I leant over the box for a peek.

"Yep, every single one," she frowned, tentatively lifting a length of tinsel and hearing the plinking and plonking of slivers of glass fall off it and tip-tap on the bottom of the box.

"Hold it *right* there!"

That was Linn swinging into action, turning super-sensible in the face of a sharp, pointy crisis.

"Put that tinsel down, *right* now, Ro! Don't touch *anything*!" she ordered our startled sister, who immediately did what she was told, for fear of being shot at dawn for disobedience. (No matter how pretty Linn is, no matter that she is only seventeen; there is *definitely* something sergeant major-ish about that girl.)

"What's wrong?" asked Tor, coming back into the living room, trailed by Rolf, who was obviously too stupid to realize he was in everybody's bad books and was supposed to be staying out in the hall as punishment.

"The decorations are too dangerous," Linn announced darkly, staring at the box as if it was an unexploded bomb or something.

"The Decorations are Too Dangerous!": it kind of sounded like they were about to multiply and take over the world, slashing any innocent human that crossed their glitter-speckled path...

"All the old glass baubles have smashed, Tor, and there're splinters of the stuff over all the tinsel and everywhere," I explained (less dramatically) for my brother's sake.

"It's a shame, but we'll just have to bin the lot."

"What?" Tor squeaked at Linn's pronouncement.

I felt a bit like squeaking myself. Maybe it's just a hazy memory for Tor, but for me, Ro and Linn, these decorations were a link to the past – a link to a time when Mum was around to help us put them up.

"But Tor, honey," Linn coaxed him in the sort of soothing voice that she *never* uses when she speaks to me and Rowan, "we'd never be able to shake all the tiny shards of glass out of the tinsel properly, so we can't risk pinning it up around the house and then having prickles of glass spraying all over the floor. What if we stood on some and cut ourselves?"

Tor didn't look convinced, although *I* suddenly was. I'd be so terrified of getting lacerated tootsies I'd spend the next six months stomping around the house in *wellies*.

"*Or* the pets," Linn said, cunningly changing her tack.

"What if Rolf or Winslet or one of the cats cut their paws?".

"Oh, OK," Tor nodded, seeing (pet-shaped) sense.

"And I guess the decorations *are* all a bit tatty anyway," I chipped in, screwing my nose up at the mangy, threadbare mound of tinsel.

"But what about the angel?" Tor suddenly announced in a panic, bolting for the box.

The angel... Mum made the angel for the first ever Christmas tree her and Dad had (about 20 centimetres high, made of plastic) in their first ever flat (about 20 centimetres wide, the way Mum described it). After realizing that a) they had about £2.50 to spend on Christmas, and b) they were living in a drab basement flat with all the charm and warmth of a disused rabbit hutch, our very-pregnant-with-Linn Mum dug out all her old art stuff and made the angel out of coloured Fimo clay. She was a very cute and fat black fairy, as the only Fimo Mum had left was brown (for the skin), black (for the hair) and white (for the tutu and wings). The reason she was fat, Dad said, was that Mum felt so huge with her baby bump that she wasn't in the mood to see anyone skinny, even on the top of their mini Christmas tree.

"Stop!" Linn barked, before Tor got a chance to dive into the box and mutilate himself. "Get the rubber gloves from the kitchen and I'll get the angel out before we chuck this lot!"

In a flash, he was gone, followed by a furry, barking blur that was Rolf.

"We can get new decorations!" Rowan chirruped,

cheering up now at the thought of a spending spree. "They always have lovely stuff up at Alexandra Palace garden centre! Last year I saw that they sprayed all these branches gold and silver and—"

"Charged a fortune," Linn butted in.

"No – not a fortune exactly," Ro tried to protest.

"But more than we can afford…"

That was me, stating the obvious. Once again, Dad's bike repair shop was going through a quiet patch (i.e. a not-exactly-making-money patch), so we could hardly go demanding cash for spangly bits when it was probably going to be a struggle for him just to get us presents, never *mind* Christmas paraphernalia. And that might include a *tree*, the way our finances were (or weren't) at the moment.

"Well, you know what Dad told us," Linn said, as she pulled on the yellow Marigold glove a breathless Tor had just handed her. "It could get busier just before Christmas, if people buy some second-hand bikes off him for presents. But we can't exactly rely on that. *Et voila!* One angel!"

Linn gave our beloved fat angel a shake and brushed her down with the dog-drool damp tissue that Ro passed helpfully to her.

"I'll go and get a black plastic rubbish bag to put this whole lot into," I muttered, getting to my feet as a useful thought entered my head.

For a second there, I thought Rolf was going to follow me. (He likes to accompany anyone leaving the living room, just in case they might be going near the fridge, or any kind of food.) But today – as if he felt somehow responsible – he stayed close by Tor's side, hunkered down on our ratty rug.

"Well, at least we've got the angel – that's all that matters. And *I* can make new decorations!" I heard Rowan sigh happily, as I left the room.

Omigod. It would be fine if Rowan just dismantled some of the reams of fairy lights from inside her room and spread them out around the house a little. But if she made them, what would they be, knowing her strange take on arts and crafts? Would we have garlands of ring-pulls twinkling above the mantelpiece? Baubles made out of ping-pong balls painted with leftover nail varnish? An angel at the top of the tree made from a cut-out picture of Kylie Minogue draped in a bit of old net curtain?

"Prrrrp!" prrrrped Colin in all his ginger glory, as he woke up from a catnap on the stairs, probably dreaming dreams of having four legs instead of just the three to bound around on.

"Go back to sleep," I whispered, scratching his twitching ears through the bannister. "There's nothing going on that you need to worry about…"

Famous last words.

Colin and I jerked to attention at the sound of three voices in unison roaring "*Rolf!*", before a thunder of paws sent Colin leaping through the bannister as our dopey dog tore past him on the stairs.

"What happened?" I asked, bursting back into the living room and trying to prise Colin's petrified claws out of my chest as he clung on for dear life. (I appreciated the fact that he'd immediately turned to me for comfort, but puncture wounds in the skin are *so* not a good look.)

Nobody answered me, but I just had to check out their faces to see that something was badly wrong. And then I spotted her; or what was left of her. Rolf had chewed up our angel – then spat out lumps of her when he realized she wasn't made out of marzipan or bread or dog food or anything else digestible.

Now we had no tree, no decorations, and no Mum-made angel.

Merry Christmas, Rolf, and thanks a lot...

Chapter 2

SNOW BALLS? (S)NO(W) THANKS...

"Don't you feel just *totally* Christmassy?" Chloe sighed happily.

Ha. Something told me that *she* hadn't had a mad dog destroy her family's entire collection of decorations in one fell swoop at the weekend...

"Um, why exactly are we standing out here again?" Salma shivered, turning up the collar of her blazer as her olive skin turned faintly blue with cold.

"Because it's pretty," Chloe replied, glancing around the snow-covered yard that was untouched and perfect five minutes ago at the start of break.

I glanced around at the chaos of zillions of boys now careering about, making slides and slapping snow in each other's faces like icy custard pies, and felt I should mention to Chloe that it would have been just as pretty looking out at it from inside the centrally-heated corridor. But funnily enough, I didn't say that out loud.

"Can we go in soon?" asked Jen, her teeth chattering out a Flamenco rhythm like castanets. Poor Jen: she had this snowman look about her, her face frozen white and her beady little dark eyes like pebbles. She didn't have a carrot for a nose though; more like a little red radish.

"God, you lot are such wimps, aren't you?" Chloe said

☆ 14 ☆

scornfully, passing Jen a tissue to dab her dripping nose.

I don't know if the weather in Ireland gets especially cold, but Chloe Brennan *had* to have some hardy genes floating around her body, courtesy of her Irish ancestry, to stand there without gloves or a scarf or a coat on over her blazer and not feel pneumonia setting in, like the rest of us were. Kellie was hugging herself so hard you'd think she was scared bits of her would fall off (through frostbite?) if she let go. My best friend Sandie was standing by my side, although it was hard to tell it was really her since all you could see above the top of her coat and scarf and under her yanked-down beanie hat was a pair of blinking, plate-sized blue eyes, with icicles hanging off her long lashes (well, *practically*).

Me? Well, I was distracting myself from the bitter cold by having a huge rant in my head about what a total *drip* I was for never standing up to Chloe. Don't get me wrong – it's not that Chloe was acting like a bully or anything; it's just that she had this determined way about her. While us lot were great at faffing around and shrugging and not making a decision on *anything*, Chloe would come out with "Right! *This* is what we're going to do!" and, like little sheep, the rest of us would all trot meekly after her. And then today, as soon as the break bell went, Chloe was leading us straight out here into the schoolyard to check out the snow that had settled while we'd been falling asleep in our Monday morning classes. Fine, except what the *rest* of us really wanted to do was get a coffee, hug a radiator and gossip about the weekend. Only we didn't say that.

Well, Jen and Salma might have been brave enough (frozen enough) to stand up to Chloe just now, but it was hopeless, really. We all knew we'd go back in when *Chloe* was ready to go back in, and it didn't seem like that was any time soon.

"So what about this charity fashion show thing?" she chattered happily, while offering around a packet of chewing gum. (None of us took any, mainly because it was too Arctic to take our hands out of our pockets.)

The charity fashion show "thing" had come up at assembly this morning. Our headteacher, Mr Bashir, said that instead of a Christmas show or concert this year, he and some of the other teachers had come up with this idea of staging a fashion show, which would be organized (and modelled) by us, and which would raise money for local charities. The money was going to come from ticket sales to watch the show, i.e. the audience was going to be made up of all of us who weren't cool enough to be part of the organizational team or glamorous enough to model. Oh, and of course the members of our families we'd suckered into buying tickets...

"Where are they going to get the clothes from?" came a muffled voice from somewhere behind Sandie's scarf.

"Stores in the area will lend them – that's what Mr Bashir said," Kellie reminded her, while shivering so much that the frost sparkled on her rows of black braids.

"Which means it's *bound* to be naff stuff, if the teachers have anything to do with it," Salma smirked.

"Maybe that Pound shop on Wood Green High Street will lend pop socks or something!" I managed to joke (even if I couldn't smirk like Salma, since my face was frozen solid).

"Yeah, but there's that other part of the show Mr Bashir was talking about," Chloe pointed out. "The themed section, where people get to design and model their own stuff!"

You could tell Mr Bashir had come up with this at the last minute, to try and keep all us non-organizational, non-modelling types interested. There'd be a competition, he'd said, to come up with a theme for the design-an-outfit section. Whoever came up with the winning theme would get to strut their stuff on stage with all the wannabe Kate Mosses and Marcus Schenkenbergs.

"What about it?" Jen squeaked miserably, huddling up to Salma for warmth.

"Well, we should come up with a theme and try and win the competition!" Chloe flashed her green eyes at Jen, as if she was being especially dumb instead of just too cold to care.

"What about a theme of recycling?" I suggested.

"Recycling?" Chloe perked up, glad to see that one of her friends was showing some enthusiasm instead of just whimpering and whingeing. "How would that work?"

"Well, like recycling old duvets into full-length, padded coats, and lining them with hot-water bottles..."

It was only a rubbish dig (the best I could manage at this temperature), but it hit the spot. Chloe looked mildly huffy, while my other mates grinned and muttered, "Oh, yes, *please*!"

"OK, OK! I get the message! We'll go back inside!"

Chloe sighed, leading the way to the side door that would take us back into the roast-toasty warm school.

"*Yessss!*" a grateful Kellie mouthed silently behind Chloe's back, giving me a high-five.

It was at that moment that I thought I heard my name being called – but with all the yelling and shouting going on in the yard it was hard to be sure. Then I heard it again, and so did Sandie, whose blue eyes fixed questioningly on mine. Together we both turned round to see which boy's voice was shouting my name and *why* exactly.

Wish I hadn't bothered. As soon as I turned, a hard-packed snowball hit me slap-bang on the boob. Ouch...

"Wow! I think that was Keith Brownlow!" Sandie exclaimed from under her layers of wool.

I didn't really care which of the now laughing bunch of lads in the year above us had chucked that snowball, all I knew was that I was hurt – more in the pride department than in the boob department. Keith Brownlow and his mates were pretty cool. I wasn't aware that they knew I existed, never mind knew my name. But what good was that, when all I was to them was target practice?

"Are you all right, Ally?" Chloe called out in concern from the open side door.

"Yeah, sure," I lied through gritted teeth as I walked towards her.

Although I guess I *was* all right, apart from the pneumonia, the frostbite, the fact that one boob was probably stunted for life after being so rudely *thunked*, and the fact that I'd been humiliated in front of half the school by a bunch of older boys.

Now what was Chloe saying earlier about feeling Christmassy...?

THE JOYS OF FESTIVE FIGHTING

You know, ever since I got thunked by that snowball yesterday morning, I'd been a touch on the paranoid side.

It was like just now; there I was, happily ambling (OK, hurrying – it was still freezing) along the street towards my house when these two little girls passed by, giggling. I got all twitchy – immediately thinking they were giggling at *me* – and did a quick check for biscuit crumbs around my mouth. (Doing my homework round Sandie's house always involves major biscuit consumption.)

Then once they'd passed me, I whipped around and saw that they were actually giggling at some balding, stocky, grumpy-looking guy waddling down the road with his canine twin – a stocky, grumpy-looking bulldog. See what I mean about being paranoid? But no sooner did I get over *that* than I spotted Mr and Mrs Fitzpatrick – the most miserable old people in the universe – standing on the pavement outside our house and tutting to each other loudly. Straight away, I assumed they were tutting at how askew I was wearing my school tie or how delinquent the badges on my blazer were. You may think I was overreacting a smidge, but no *way*: it was well known in our neighbourhood that Mr and Mrs Fitzpatrick disliked and disapproved of the world at large, i.e. they got off on doing stuff like putting nasty notes on the cars of anyone who parked or *sneezed* within a 20 kilometre radius of their precious disabled space, even though no one knew what they were supposed to be disabled *by*, apart from pure spite, of course. But Mr and Mrs Fitzpatrick *particularly* disliked and disapproved of the Love family. Our crimes were:

1) Four of us happened to be children. (They were allergic to children.)

2) We weren't "normal" (i.e. Mum wasn't around any more).

3) We were never going to win any awards for best-kept home and garden. (Hey, we like the lived-in look.)

4) We had pets (which carry germs).

5) We lived next door to them (probably carrying germs ourselves).

Shocking, I know.

But on this occasion, paranoia had won out again; on closer inspection, Mr and Mrs Fitzpatrick *weren't* tut-tutting at me, but at the front of our house for some reason.

"Hello!" I tried to say brightly, forcing a fake smile on to my face. ("Always be polite to obnoxious people," Mum once told us. "It always confuses them.")

"Hurumph!" grumbled Mr Fitzpatrick.

"Ridiculous!" grumbled Mrs Fitzpatrick.

Then both of them bumbled off along the pavement with their cloud of gloom hovering over them, leaving a vapour trail of bad vibes in their wake.

Coughing slightly, I opened our creaky front gate

(decorated with more rust than paint), then got bedazzled with the wondrousness of my sister Rowan's Christmas handicraft... Other people might soon be hanging wreaths of holly leaves and ivy on their front door, but ours was rather more interesting and unique than that (and Mr and Mrs Fitzpatrick didn't approve of "interesting" and "unique"). Our wreath was made out of an old, pink, feather boa wrapped around a circle of wire, with delicate white fairy lights intertwined and blinking out from underneath the feathers.

"Ro?" I called out as I pushed open the front door, dying to ask her which second-hand store she'd got the boa from.

But Rowan couldn't hear me calling out her name because she and Linn were arguing too loudly in the kitchen.

"Don't ask, Ally..." Grandma rolled her eyes as she wandered upstairs with a bundle of newly ironed clothes in her arms. "I've got to help Tor with his homework after I've put this lot away, so I haven't got time to play referee. Can you try and calm your sisters down before your father comes home to all this mayhem?"

"Um, OK," I said nervously, watching Grandma stride upstairs and out of view. "But you've got to give me a clue – what are they rowing about?"

"Something about a fashion show at school," she shrugged, obviously well fed-up with today's bickering session already.

I gulped, hung up my coat, dumped my bag, stepped over a snoozly Winslet and Rolf and dived into the fray.

"Hey! What's up?"

It's hard to sound casual when you're walking into a war zone, but I had to try. At least it got the two of them to shut up for a split-second. Both my sisters turned to face me, looking about as opposite as people can get. (Linn groomed, blondish and immaculate in black trousers and black polo neck; Rowan … well, Rowan was looking "interesting" and "unique", as always).

"What's *up*," Linn began to moan to her audience of one (me), "is that *I'm* on the committee for the fashion show at school, and I've just found out that *bird-brain* here is too!"

You know, I really don't like it when Linn has a go at Rowan for being an airhead (which she is), but a small part of me did see her problem with Ro being involved in the organizational side of things, since Rowan is the least organized person I know. (I mean, red clogs, black woolly tights, kid's kilt worn as a mini, dayglo yellow mohair jumper and a giant daisy clip in her brown hair – not exactly organized, is it?)

"What are you both in charge of, then?" I asked as cheerfully as possible.

"*I'm* in charge of getting stores to lend clothes, amongst other things," Linn responded.

"And *I'm* in charge of set design," said Rowan hotly, her cheeks flushed an indignant pink.

"Which is going to be a *total* disaster, since she'll probably want to turn the hall stage into a cross between the set of *The Nutcracker* ballet and the underwater scene in *The Little Mermaid*!"

Rowan blinked a little at Linn, thrown off track by the fact that she quite liked that idea.

"And when it comes to money," Linn leapt in again, "Tor's *stick* insects have a better grasp of budgets than you do, Rowan. I'd be better asking *them* for costings for this project than you!"

Uh-oh … it was one of those moments when Rowan is on the cusp, in that danger zone between arguing back and bursting into tears. I had to do something to distract her, and *fast*.

"Hey, *love* that thing you made for the front door, Ro!"

"Do you, Ally?" Ro's face lit up instantly with my compliment. "I got the boa from that charity shop on Tottenham Lane that's really good. And I used one of my strings of fairy lights from around my bed-head to make—"

"Whoa!" Linn interrupted, holding her hands palms-up in front of her. "These fairy lights – are they the outdoor or indoor type?"

Ro scrunched her eyes up in confusion, as if Linn had just asked her to describe the purpose of quantum physics or something.

"Are they for outdoor use or indoor use only, Ro!" Linn repeated, her pert nostrils flaring ominously.

"*I* don't know!" Rowan shrugged. "What difference does it make?"

"What *difference* does it make?"

Linn's pale eyebrows had levitated halfway up her forehead in surprise at our sister's ignorance. I didn't dare open my mouth and say I wasn't really sure what the problem was either...

"Ro, if they're made for outdoor use, there's no problem. But if they're indoor use only, they'll probably burst into flames when the first snowflake hits them and then – *whoosh!* – the next thing any of us know, the fire brigade will be round here trying to drag us out of a burning building. Get my point?"

I think Rowan definitely got Linn's point, from the way she went zooming out of the kitchen door, bottom lip trembling, mumbling something about going to her room.

"I've had enough of this," Linn growled, stomping off towards the stairs too, and the sanctity of her own neat, uncluttered, fairy-light-free room up in the attic.

Phew – at least the two of them had stopped fighting for a while, well before Dad arrived home (no thanks to me, of course). After that little burst of excitement, I decided I needed to do some serious flopping on the sofa with whichever cat was handy.

"Coming through for a cuddle?" I asked a cat that wasn't Colin, who was presently settling down to sleep on my schoolbag in the hall.

Then I noticed the wire wending it's way under the front door and ending in a plug on the wall – which I bent over and flicked off just to be on the safe side. (I didn't want Dad coming home to a real home fire, if you see what I mean.)

So much for my sofa-flopping plans – Tor had already beaten me to it.

"What're you doing?" I asked, plonking myself down next to him.

"Homework," he mumbled, twirling a rubber chicken-topped pencil around in his fingers.

"Why's your book upside-down, then?"

"Oh."

Tor twirled his book the right way round but didn't seem any keener on actually writing anything down in it.

"Something up, Tor?"

The thing is, when there *is* something up with our seven-year-old brother, it's very hard to tell, since he gives so few clues. I tell you, it would be very useful to be psychic sometimes...

Tor gazed his Malteser eyes up at me and uttered one, soulful word.

"Play."

"Play?" I repeated, frantically trying to figure out what he was on about.

"It's his school's Nativity play," Grandma usefully explained, bustling into the room, smacking her hands together now her chores were done. "His teacher's given him the part of Joseph, but he's not happy about it. Are you, sweetheart?"

Tor shook his head sadly, and I frowned over the top of it at Grandma, who shrugged back at me, evidently just as puzzled as me at why Mrs Halston had decided to give one of the quietest kids at school one of the biggest parts in the school play. I dunno – maybe she thought doing the play would bring Tor out of himself or something. But I had a sneaking suspicion that all that was going to happen was that there would be a lot of long, empty silences on the day of their performance...

"Tor, tell your sister which part you *really* wanted," Grandma encouraged him, with a quick wink in my direction through her gold-framed specs.

A blissful expression flitted across his face, similar to the zen-like trance Rowan goes into if you dangle something shiny and pretty in front of her.

"One of the sheep," he sighed.

"Or one half of a donkey," Grandma chipped in.

"Don't mind which end!" said Tor enthusiastically.

"Ally, you're not involved in any Christmas shows, are you, dear?"

"Nope." I shook my head at Grandma's question.

"Oh, good. Between your sisters and this one, I think it's going to be a very stressful run up to the end of term..."

Although I was smiling at Grandma's little jokette, I had the funniest feeling in my stomach as soon as she said that. It took a second to figure out what it was, and then I realized it was plain, old-fashioned jealousy. Tor, Linn and Rowan were all doing Important Stuff, and I felt left out, even though I knew that was dumb, considering one of them wanted to be a sheep and not Joseph and the other two were probably going to end up killing each other. (If Rowan's home-made Christmas decorations didn't end up killing us all first.)

This was no good. Having a bad case of left-out-ness coupled with a decoration-free house was no way to get in a festive mood. Starting tomorrow, I decided, I was going to *throw* myself physically into the Christmas spirit. Maybe I'd go window shopping for presents after school. Or build a snowman in the garden. Or even get revenge for my bruised boob and chuck a snowball at Keith oh-so-cool Brownlow.

When he wasn't looking, of course. (Hey, I'm not *that* brave...)

Chapter 4

A NIGHT WITH RACHEL'S TROUSERS...

It was Wednesday, it was officially my first day trying to get into the Christmas spirit, and so far I'd been doing OK – I'd put my hands over my ears and hummed "Silent Night" when Linn and Rowan started arguing at breakfast (got butter and toast crumbs in my hair, of course); I ran giggling through deep snow on my way to school (and had to sit through three classes till my feet dried out); bought some Christmas cards at lunchtime (bit of a drag when I found out Sandie had bought exactly the same design); and was now round at Jen's for a Girls' Video Night (pity the Christmas-themed movie we were watching was so schmaltzy it was making us all *barf*).

Luckily, Jen's older sister Rachel stuck her head around the door and interrupted us. It was a relief to have an excuse to hit the pause button.

"Hey, Jen – can I borrow your denim shirt?"

Picture this: you get in some kind of time machine doodah and zap three years into the future, and there's your thirteen-year-old friend as her more grown-up sixteen-year-old self. Well, that's what it's like looking at Rachel; she's *spookily* similar to Jen (same mannerisms, same fair, shoulder-length hair, same teeny-tiny button-round eyes). It's not just a vague family resemblance –

like I've got with Rowan and Tor, and even Linn a little bit – it's as if the two of them are twins gone wonky or something.

"Yeah, sure, Rach," Jen shrugged, grabbing another handful of Hula Hoops from the bowl on the floor. "It's in my wardrobe. Help yourself."

Wow. Amazing. If I asked to borrow anything of Linn's I'd be laughed out of the house. And then she'd say no. If I asked to borrow anything of Rowan's, then I'd be *mad*...

"You're going to let her borrow that denim shirt you just bought?" Chloe frowned at Jen as soon as the door had shut behind Rachel. "You haven't even worn that yet!"

"I know," Jen shrugged, wiping her salty fingers on her jeans. "But it's OK – she's lending me her velvet trousers for the school Christmas disco in two weeks' time."

"Those black velvet flares?" Salma asked in amazement.

We'd all flipped over the black velvet flares last time it was Jen's turn for a Girls' Video Night. It was a Saturday and Rachel had strode into the living room in search of her watch on her way out to a party. Five seconds previously, we'd all been drooling over Ryan Phillippe on screen, and suddenly we were all drooling over the coolest pair of trousers in the universe. We talked more about them ("Where did she get them from?"; "*How* much did they cost?") than the film for the rest of the evening.

"Yes," Jen nodded proudly, "she's lending me her flares."

"In return for a loan of your denim shirt? *That*'s not bad!" I commented.

Jen began to squirm, and I don't think it was just 'cause her bum was going numb sitting on the polished wood floor.

"Well, it's not *just* the shirt. I've also had to promise to do her turn of the hoovering for the whole of December..."

"That's not *too* awful," Kellie told her. (Since Kellie had no brothers or sisters to share housework duty with, I'm sure it *didn't* seem too awful.)

"...*and* I've had to lend her my CD Walkman, since hers is broken and she isn't getting a new one till Christmas..."

"Oh," mumbled Sandie dubiously.

"...*and* I promised that instead of us taking turns to do it, *I'll* clean out the cat litter tray."

"How long for?" Chloe wrinkled up her nose in disgust.

"For ever."

Chloe stuck her fingers down her throat and mimed barfing big-time.

So let's see... A loan of a denim shirt, a month's worth of hoovering, the temporary loss of a CD Walkman and a lifetime's worth of cat poo = one night with Rachel's trousers.

"Still..." said Salma, as we all mentally weighed up the deal. "You get to wear the velvet flares to the party!"

The school Christmas party: we were all pretty excited about that. For some reason (probably because it was cheaper or something), Mr Bashir had announced that *this* time round, our year and the year above would be having a combined do. Instantly – for everyone in our year – that made the party a whole lot more exciting. (Even though it probably made the whole of the year above us *groan*.)

"Hey, Jen – you'll probably have all the older boys fighting over you in those trousers!" Sandie grinned.

"Well, all of them except Keith Brownlow," Chloe narrowed her eyes wickedly in my direction. "He'll be chatting up Ally, since he fancies her so much!"

It was such a stupid, ridiculous thing for her to say that I felt my face flush red and my tongue tie in knots.

"He does *not*... I mean, he *hit* me!" I protested, while all my friends started disloyally sniggering.

"He hit you with a *snowball*, Ally, so that's not exactly assault," said Chloe, leaning over and making a grab for the bag she'd brought with her. "*And* he knew your name. He's *bound* to fancy you!"

"Look, we're not at primary school!" I argued back. "It's not like some little boy has thumped me on the arm or nicked my doll 'cause he likes me!"

"Near enough." Chloe shrugged infuriatingly, acting like she'd had years of experience with lads when she'd exactly the same total of boyfriends as me, i.e. *none*. "Anyway, why don't we turn that rubbish movie off and try and think up some ideas for that fashion show competition?"

"Oh, yes!" Salma perked up enthusiastically, same as Kellie, Sandie and Jen. "That'd be fun. The closing date's this Friday, isn't it?"

It's amazing: one minute, your so-called mates are entertaining themselves by watching you squirm in embarrassment, the next you're left with blazing cheeks while they swan off in a different direction, conversationally speaking.

"Yep," nodded Chloe, pulling a notepad and pen out of her bag. "And I've had a few ideas so far. How about –"

She paused, her eyes scanning her scribbled notes as her fingers pushed her red hair behind her ears. (OK, so her hair's actually *ginger*, but we're never, *never* allowed to call it that on pain of death.)

"– a *snowman* theme?"

The smiles faded from my other friends' faces.

"Snowmen? Are you *sure*?" Salma asked bluntly.

"Yeah! What's wrong with that?" Chloe mumbled huffily.

"So in that section of the fashion show, everyone is meant to design and model a costume based on *snowmen*?" Sandie asked, looking puzzled and concerned.

It was now Chloe's turn to blush, her flame red cheeks clashing with her marmalade red hair, now that everyone was pointing out the naffness of her idea. I mean, could you imagine if Mr Bashir announced that as the winning theme? Precisely *no one* would enter a design for that. Not even *Rowan* would be crazy enough to waddle around on the stage dressed as a snowman in front of the entire school and expect to come out of it with her pride intact.

"But it's a good Christmas theme, isn't it?" Chloe bleated on, not exactly willing to dump her daft suggestion.

"Yeah, but so's the Three Wise Men, and no one would want to dress up as *them*!" I teased her, immediately thinking about Tor and his Nativity play. "And so's Santa Claus, and reindeer, and angels at the top of the tree, but no one's going to want to put on padding and fake beards and red noses and—"

"Angels!" Chloe interrupted my witterings. "That's it, Ally – angels!"

My first thought was that she was crazy, mainly because the Christmas angel I had in my mind was a fat Fimo fairy that was currently in chewed bits at the bottom of a bin bag round the side of our house. Then as the other girls started gasping and chattering, I realized that I'd had a Very Good Idea. Even if it *was* by accident.

"It'd be such a pretty theme – *loads* of people will want to enter designs for it!" Chloe cooed. "Can you imagine? All those acres of lace and glitter and stuff? God, this is *bound* to win!"

Bound to win... Good grief, could you imagine if we *did* win? Could you imagine one of us actually getting the chance to go up on stage and model? Could you imagine if that one of us was *me*, wafting around in some beautiful, floaty creation?

"Ally, why are you blushing?" I heard Jen suddenly ask, which made me blush even more.

But how could I tell her about the vision I'd just had? The vision of Linn's best mate Alfie – ridiculously *gorgeous* Alfie – sitting in the audience, staring up at me through the darkness as I sashayed around on the spotlit stage. Normally, thanks to my jeans and trainers and acute embarrassment in his presence, he never really seemed to know I existed. But if I had an angel make-over, could he maybe, possibly, *hopefully* fall for me?

Of course not.

But – for the second year running – that wasn't going to stop me hoping that Santa would leave me a boyfriend-shaped present under the tree. A boyfriend-shaped present called Alfie...

WEIRD DREAMS AND DAFT DOGS

For the last two nights – since the Girls' Video Night round at Jen's – I'd had the strangest recurring dreams. They'd started the same way: I'd be all dressed up, waiting to go out on a date with Alfie. This wasn't so strange – I regularly dream daydreams and night-dreams about Alfie (dating him, holding hands with him, snogging the face off him), but the weird thing about these dreams was that I was dressed up as an angel, which wasn't too ideal if all we were going to do was go for a walk in the park or share a chicken nugget or three at KFC.

Then the dreams got *seriously* weird. In Wednesday night's version, Alfie turned up – all blond and cheek-bones and irresistible as ever – and as we strolled out of the house (difficult with angel wings getting stuck in the doorway), he turned around to talk to me and had suddenly morphed into Keith Brownlow. Eeek!

If that wasn't weird enough, on Thursday night, I got to the same leaving-the-house point, and when Alfie turned around, this time he'd morphed into my boy buddy Billy, which was very, *very* blah indeed. I mean, the idea of going out on a date with Billy! I'd rather date Rolf – he's cuter...

Both nights, I woke up with a start, and had to put my

bedside light on to calm down (which didn't go down well with the rudely awakened selection of pets that were sharing my room and bed, let me tell you).

"You look terrible," Sandie said, as she eyed me sympathetically at break-time today. "Are you OK, Ally?"

Nice one, Sandie, I thought to myself. *You score ten-out-of-ten for being a top-notch caring friend, but you'll have to do some homework if you want to get your grades up in the subject of Tact...*

"Just haven't been sleeping," I mumbled.

I probably *would* tell Sandie later what had been keeping me awake – she was coming back to mine for tea – but I didn't want to bring up my pathetic dating dreams in front of my other mates. Alfie fantasies aside, I'd just *hate* to come across as one of those wimpy girls who were always gagging to have a boyfriend or something. Why should I be? The only two of my friends who *had* dated didn't have exactly fantastic experiences. Salma went out with David Ling for four weeks and had about three private conversations with him in all that time, since every date seemed to include at least two of his mates tagging along like great big lemons. Then there was Jen; her boyfriend Gavin thought it was OK to mention casually which other girls he happened to fancy. Mmm, very flattering for Jen. *Not...*

"Oh, here comes Chloe now," said Kellie, pointing up the packed corridor as Chloe scurried towards us.

"Where have you been?" asked Jen. "You just vanished when we went to buy crisps!"

"Yeah – I just remembered that I should drop off that

angel idea we had for the fashion show," Chloe replied, nicking a crisp out of Jen's open bag. "It was the closing day today, remember."

Um, no, I don't think any of us *had* remembered. It was pretty organized of Chloe to bother to write that suggestion out neatly and hand it in for us.

"So what's up with you today, Ally?" Chloe turned to me, with a mouth full of crisps. "You look terrible!"

"Well, thanks," I muttered sarcastically. "I just didn't sleep very well."

"No – I meant *that*!"

I glanced down where she was pointing and saw a gaping hole where the knee of my black, woolly tights should be.

"Rolf…" I growled, holding my leg out straight in front of me to examine the damage. You could practically *see* the teeth marks, where he'd chewed my knee when I was attempting to leave the house this morning. Because I'd woken up with a fringe that was pointing in all directions of the compass, I'd had to do some emergency blow-drying. Then I'd realized that both pairs of school trousers were in the wash, and had to stick on a stupid skirt, by which time I was so super-late that all I had time for was disengaging Rolf's teeth from my knee and I didn't bother to inspect the damage. I'd *wondered* why it was so breezy about the leg department when I was running to school…

"Is he still eating everything that isn't nailed down?" Salma grinned at me.

"Yep. Rowan came home with a bunch of pine cones

she collected from Queen's Woods yesterday," I explained, letting Sandie and Jen take a turn at examining my knee. "She was going to spray them with leftover bike paint from Dad's shop; y'know – to make decorations, but she left them on the kitchen table for five minutes and when she came back, all she heard was the sound of Rolf crunching the last one."

It was odd, really. Winslet was the one who usually liked to chew or steal anything she could reach – which wasn't much, since her legs were so short her fuzzy belly practically skimmed the floor. Rolf tended to stick to eating dog food and any human food he could trick us out of. This current bad habit of trashing our house was making him the least popular pet at 28 Palace Heights Road, for sure. Well, except where Tor was concerned. He'd forgive an animal anything. A crocodile could bite Tor's arm off and he'd probably see the funny side.

"Why did Rolf attack your knee?"

"Did he break the skin?"

"No, he was just playing," I answered Sandie and Jen in one fell swoop, as I continued to stand on one leg, like a flamingo in school uniform. "He's never had much of a brain, but I don't know what's going on with him just now…"

I was staring hard at the ladder that was now gaping its way down from the ripped knee of my tights when I heard a Boy Someone say my name.

"Um, Ally…"

I turned around, slamming my foot down a little too

hard in surprise. A few people close by visibly flinched at the loud *thwack* my black school shoe made on contact with the corridor's lino.

"Hello?" I mumbled uncertainly to Ben Something-Or-Other, as I racked my memory banks for his last name, and wondered in a panic what he could want with me.

"Um… I'm mates with Keith. Keith Brownlow. And he asked me to ask you…"

Instantly, the world slowed down all around me. I'm not a big-head, I'm not presumptuous, I couldn't actually *believe* this was happening to me when I'd spent the last few minutes talking about my mental dog while holding my leg in the air like a lunatic, but omigod – I was about to be asked out, if I wasn't wildly, madly, *insanely* deluded.

"…Keith was just wondering, like, if you…"

Ben Something-Or-Other had an awkward grin on his face, as if he'd taken on this job of messenger as a funny dare and was now finding it more embarrassing than he'd expected.

"…if you'd be up for going out with him. 'Cause he fancies you and everything."

Well, I'd *hope* it was 'cause he fancied me – if he wanted to go out with me because he *hated* me I'd have to *really* worry about his sanity and my safety.

It was only when I felt a tiny nudge in my back from Sandie that I realized that I was now expected to say something in response. In a panic, I looked fleetingly around at my girlfriends for inspiration, but found only four stunned and grinning faces (Sandie, Jen, Kellie and Salma), and one stunned and *frosty* face (Chloe). What was all that about? Right now, the world had gone too weird to worry about a detail like that.

"Yes. OK. Fine. OK. Yeah, I would. Go out with him, I mean," I heard a voice witter dumbly. How *shamed* am I that it was mine.

"OK. Fine. I'll tell him," smirked Ben Something-Or-Other.

And he walked away, leaving me wondering what on earth was supposed to happen next, apart from my knees turning to pure custard and me crumbling to the floor in a fainting pile of panic.

"Help?" I muttered in the direction of my mates as soon as Ben Something-Or-Other wandered off.

Salma, Sandie and Kellie looked too stunned to say anything. Chloe looked too strangely grumpy to say anything. Luckily, Jen piped up with just the right thing.

"Crisp?"

"Thank you…" I said gratefully, helping myself to her packet.

Y'see, you might not know where you are with boys and emotions, but you always know where you are with salt and vinegar crisps…

Chapter 6

FIRST TIME, FAST TIME

Speak about icebergs ... all day yesterday, Chloe went very cool on me. It freaked me out, to tell you the truth. I mean, it wasn't as if she *fancied* Keith Brownlow or anything, so why the big, silent strop? I couldn't figure it out, and neither could Sandie, when we spent the whole of Friday night discussing it.

And the funny thing is, Chloe's not the only one who doesn't fancy Keith Brownlow – neither do I. But what are you meant to do when a coolish, OK-looking, year-older lad asks you out?

"You've got to go," Sandie told me in no uncertain terms last night, as we sat in bed (me in mine, Sandie on the inflatable mattress on the floor of my room). "Even if it's just for the experience!"

It's very hard to take someone seriously when they're prattling on about getting "experience" in dating when they're wearing pyjamas with Winnie-the-Pooh on them. I've got nothing against Winnie-the-Pooh – it's one of my favourite things to read with Tor ("Read me the bit where Pooh's so fat he gets stuck in the doorway!") – but I couldn't really take emotional advice from Sandie seriously till she repeated it to me in sensible clothes.

And dating Keith Brownlow? Was that going to be

sensible? Well, heaps of girls in my year thought he was plenty cute enough. He was centre forward in his year's school football team; he hung around with a cool bunch of guys (including Ben Something-Or-Other); he was legendary as being the first guy in his year to get to level five of *Digi-Kong III*.

OK, so heaps of girls I knew fancied him for all that. But Truth-Time: I didn't actually know what a centre forward did (was central? but forward?); I had no idea why anyone thought Keith and Ben Something-Or-Other or the other lads they hung about with were particularly cool; and I made up the thing about him getting to level five of *Digi-Kong III*. May God – or my PlayStation-fixated friend Billy – strike me down here for my ignorance, but I am glaringly ignorant of all computer-nerd game stuff. I knew Keith Brownlow was good at something like that, but if you asked me to try and remember exactly what it was then I'd sorely disappoint you.

"Ever played *Grand Theft Auto*?"

"Um, no..." I told Keith Brownlow, too scared to even look at him, as we bumbled through Priory Park, after meeting outside the paddling pond, as pre-agreed with Ben Something-Or-Other, when he came running back to me yesterday at break with the details of my First Date With Keith (which Ben had managed to forget to tell me when he first asked me for a date by proxy).

"It's great! It's this game where you nick cars and..."

Blah, blah, blah. This is the sort of thing my best mate Billy tries to talk to me about, but at least I can tell him to shut up and get a life. When you're on your first official date you're not allowed to do that, I don't think.

"What about *Hooligan*? Have you played that?"

"No..." I shake my head, sneaking a quick look at Keith Brownlow out of school uniform this Saturday afternoon. He's pretty presentable, with a zip-up fleecy top and cargo pants on. He shouldn't have worn trainers, though. Not with this amount of slushy, semi-icy snow about.

"It's great! It was banned, and then not banned, and then banned, but whatever, I've got this pirate copy, and it's about all these football hooligans and they— Urgh!"

Keith and his slippy trainers nearly took a dive on to the ground, which wouldn't have been too cool in front of me, or the elderly dog-walkers and two year olds running about in wellies in the fast-melting snow all around us.

"Yeah, I'm fine, it's OK," he said, blushing if I saw right, as I stuck my arm under his to stop him falling. "What about *Rez*? Have you done *Rez*? I got that off my mate today. We swap stuff all the time: old games, new games, it's brilliant."

"No, I haven't done *Rez*," I told Keith, wondering if I dared confess to him that our house was so antiquated that we didn't even have digital telly, never mind a computer. Good grief, we still didn't even have a remote, since Rolf chewed it to smithereens before I put the batteries back in. Maybe it was just as well they weren't back in: batteries are full of very toxic stuff, so Rolf might have been a bit of a poorly mental dog if that had happened.

"Pity," Keith shook his head sadly, as if I'd missed one of the wonders of the world.

And then a silence took hold … colder than any clumps of melting ice on the park land around us. I had to come out with something.

"Me and my brother went to the pet shop this morning," I heard myself say.

Good grief … there was Keith, trying to talk about cool computer games, and now here I was, trying to tell him about hamster bedding and other exciting pet requirements. Was I demented?

"Uh-huh?" muttered Keith warily.

"Yeah," I tried to squeak confidently, even though I didn't have a clue where I was going with this. "We bought Christmas dog collars for our two dogs. They weren't expensive or anything – they're just cheap and stupid. They've got this switch – when you put it on in the dark, it flashes red, on and off, a bit like Christmas tree lights."

You know, by Keith's resounding silence, I knew that wasn't the kind of conversation he wanted to have when he was out on a date.

"Hey, I can't stay long. I've got to go and see a mate," he mumbled, confirming my worst fears that I was boring him to death with my drivel about dog collars and my resounding lack of computer game knowledge.

"OK," I shrugged, wondering why I'd bothered to spend all of last night and most of today figuring out a warm yet fashionable outfit to meet him in (fake Caterpillar boots, black jeans, woolly grey polo, navy duffel coat, stripy scarf and matching gloves, look of sheer panic…).

Good grief: my first and only date was going to be over in seconds, and there'd *never* be another.

"Fancy meeting up again on Wednesday, after school? Main gates?"

"Yes," I managed to bleat, as Keith Brownlow started backing away towards a side entrance to the park.

And then he was gone. I'd had a five-minute date with a boy I didn't know if I fancied, but it couldn't have gone *too* badly, if he'd asked to meet me again.

And at least this time, I realized, he hadn't chucked a rock-hard snowball at me (or my still-bruised boob)…

Chapter 7

NOT FAIRY NICE

If I had to describe Sandie, the first thing I'd say about her is that she's kind of shy (yeah, understatement of the *year*), but she certainly isn't shy about making herself at home in my house...

"Ooh, you're back! I didn't think you'd be here for ages!" said my best friend, gazing at me from over the top of a steaming mug of hot chocolate that Rowan appeared to have just made for her.

"Yeah, well ... here I am!" I shrugged vaguely, shooting a look at Sandie that I hoped translated as: "Don't say anything about Keith in front of Rowan!"

I really like my sister – it's pretty good fun living with someone who's as batty as a very mad fruit bat – but I wasn't exactly up for sharing tales of lurve with her.

"So," said Rowan, spinning round from the sink where she was soaking the milk pan. "How did your date go?"

Great. For the price of a mug of hot chocolate, Sandie had sold my secret to my sister...

"It went ... OK," I told Rowan, feeling that familiar pink flood my cheeks. "Um, Sandie, fancy going up to my room? *Now?*"

Rowan looked faintly disappointed that she wasn't going to get any more gossip than that, while Sandie looked faintly alarmed at the stern schoolteacher tone in my voice. Instantly, she stood up to follow me, making a surprised "eek!" and then a *thump* noise as she did so. Well, maybe it was *Colin* who made the "eek!" and *thump* noises as he found himself suddenly sliding off the comfy lap he'd just settled down on and landing slap-bang on the floor.

Going out into the hall, my grumpiness left me for a second as I struggled to figure out what was different – then I spotted it: the wooden handrail of the bannister seemed to have sprouted into life. From the ground floor all the way upstairs, it was covered in leaves and berries – real ivy and holly, I thought – all tied on with garden twine. Looked like Rowan had been busy with her Christmas decorating today. It also looked like we couldn't actually *use* the handrail till January, if we didn't want to end up with prickled fingers...

"Look, I'm sorry!" Sandie hissed at me as she followed me up the stairs. (In turn, Colin was hopping after her, still determined to sit on her lap, come what may.)

"I thought you could keep a secret!" I hissed back over my shoulder, retracting my forgetful hand from the jaggedy holly leaves.

"I can! I just didn't know it *was* a secret!"

Hmm. I suppose that's fair enough.

"I just got talking to Rowan and she was telling me about her and Linn both modelling in the fashion show and—"

"They're not modelling," I corrected her. "Linn's involved in the organization side and Rowan's helping with the set design."

"Oh, I know that. But they're both modelling, too," Sandie filled me in, obviously far more knowledgeable about my family's life than I was. "Linn's going to be in the main show modelling normal clothes, and Rowan's going to be in the design-an-outfit section."

"But how does she know she's going to be entering that? They haven't even announced what the theme is yet!"

"She says she doesn't care what the theme is," Sandie replied, scooping Colin into her arms before she tripped over him. "She said she just wants to design something, that's all."

Well, she would, I guess. Rowan takes after our mum, and gets creative withdrawal symptoms if she's not painting, gluing, making, sewing or tying twigs round bannisters.

"Wonder if our angel theme will get picked, Ally? Wouldn't that be exciting?"

Considering my two sisters were not only involved in the organization of the fashion show but were now also doing their Kate Moss/Stella McCartney turns, then yes, it would be exciting if the angel theme got chosen – just so I didn't feel like the complete loser of the family. And if it didn't, then maybe I should go to Tor's teacher and see if she'd got a spare part I could play in his Nativity Show...

"Anyway, come on – tell me! How did it go with Keith?"

I'm not great at staying mad at anyone, and by the time it took us to get up to my attic bedroom (following the trail of holly and ivy all the way up), I'd completely forgotten to be grumpy with Sandie.

For the next ten minutes (i.e. five minutes longer than my date lasted), I went over every detail with her, analysing every little scrap of the conversation and the meaning behind every pause.

"They say first dates are often rubbish," Sandie concluded, with her usual well-meaning lack of tact. "'Cause of both people being nervous and everything. It'll probably be a lot better when you meet him on Wednesday."

My dating agony aunt was currently standing in my blue-painted attic room, swaying slightly as she rocked Colin in her arms. He was lying on his back, baby-style (something cats aren't meant to like, but no one had bothered to tell Colin), his one front paw lazily batting at the blow-up world globe I have dangling from my ceiling on a bit of string.

"I hope so," I murmured, biting my lip. Already I had butterflies ram-raiding their way around my stomach at the very thought of my four-days-away date.

"Oh, I meant to tell you!" Sandie suddenly perked up. (Her blue eyes are always huge at the best of times. When she's surprised or excited, they get so huge that it's like she's turning into a Japanese cartoon character before your very eyes.)

"What?"

I was quite in the mood to hear gossip that wasn't anything to do with me. I sat up straighter in my cross-legged position on my bed and was ready to receive.

"Well, it's kind of funny," Sandie began, walking over

and flopping down beside me on my cloud-covered duvet. (Colin flipped the right way round and curled himself up into a lap-sized ball of ginger fluff.) "But on my way round here, Chloe texted me, asking how your date had gone."

"Chloe? Wow!" I grinned, pleased to hear my friend was mildly intrigued about what was going on with me after her frosty mood yesterday.

"It's not *that* wow," Sandie frowned. "I texted back and said I didn't know, 'cause it hadn't happened yet. And then I told her she should call you later to find out how it went."

"And?" I frowned back. "What did she say to that?"

"She said nah, she wouldn't bother – she wasn't that interested."

"What *is* her problem?" I asked, though I knew Sandie was just as blank as me over that one.

"Maybe she's in a bad mood about other stuff, and it's just coming over like she's in a bad mood with you?" Sandie suggested.

"I dunno. I *hope* so…"

I didn't like the idea of one of my friends going weird on me for no good reason.

Maybe, I thought, *I should phone one of the others and see if they knew what*—

"God! What was that?" squeaked Sandie, as a blood-curdling yell of the Linn variety wafted up the stairs.

"Trouble," I mumbled, untangling my legs with difficulty (they'd gone to sleep) and limping over to the door and down the stairs.

The scene in Rowan's room would have been very cute, if it wasn't for a rabid Linn grovelling around on her hands and knees and ranting under Rowan's bed.

Ro's room is raspberry red and looks like an explosion in a craft shop, with glitter and spangles and sequins plastered on every surface. Once your eyes adjust to the shock, you realize that the main spangly thing in there is the miles and miles of multicoloured, dainty white and novelty-shaped fairy lights she has draped everywhere. And right now, a particularly festive set of flashing coloured lights was wrapped right around a contented-looking Tor.

"What's she doing?" I asked Rowan, who was standing staring at Linn's bent back.

Before Rowan – who was armed with a camera for some reason – could reply, Linn got in there first.

"*She*," growled Linn, straightening up as the fairy lights flashed to a darkened standstill, "was trying to find the plug so *she* could switch those lights off before our brother gets electrocuted!"

I didn't like to point out to Linn that not only was her hair escaping from the tight ponytail she had it scraped back in, but there was a large, grey, under-bed bundle of fluff attached to the side of her head. She looked angry enough as it was.

"I wasn't getting 'leccy-cuted!" Tor said indignantly, while stroking a bewildered iguana he had tucked under his arm. "Kevin was going to be on my cards!"

It's not often Tor says (almost) complete sentences, so he was obviously pretty riled, just like Linn, but for totally opposite reasons.

"I was going to take his photo, and do loads of copies to make into Christmas cards!" Rowan explained to me and Sandie, as we hovered in the doorway and surveyed the scene.

"Yeah, nice idea." Linn rolled her eyes as she got to her feet. "'Merry Christmas, from Martin Love and the kids – oh, all except the *dead* one!'"

"But I'm not dead!" Tor frowned.

"But you *could* have been!" Linn almost shouted, which made Tor flinch in alarm.

"Linn, you're scaring him!" I pointed out, hurrying over to give our brother a reassuring hug (even though the fairy lights wound around him made him about as cuddly as the holly on the bannister).

"Sorry, babes," said Linn, immediately softening. "I'm not mad at you! I'm mad at *her* for being irresponsible!"

At the sight of Linn's accusing, pointing finger, Rowan started to blub, which made Tor blub, which got Sandie going (she has an automatic cry reflex which kicks in whenever anyone else is crying), and then I started to feel slightly choked with all the emotion swirling round in the room.

"Yeah! Go ahead! Make me feel like the bad guy!" Linn sighed, then stomped out of the room with suspiciously watery eyes, for all her growling.

"She's such a grumpy moo!" Rowan snuffled.

"I *heard* that, Rowan Love!" Linn yelled out from the landing as she started to thump her way up to her own room.

Hmm. It looked like the season of goodwill might be bypassing my sisters this year, the way things were going…

Chapter 8

ANOTHER FRIEND, ANOTHER HUFF

"How does it work?" Billy interrupted what I was saying, and fiddled with the knobbly plastic collar round Winslet's neck.

"You press the switch there," I told him, bending over on the park bench and pointing at Winslet's neck.

Winslet growled at me. Gee thanks – I'm only the person that drags herself out of the house to give you long walks, you ungrateful hairy sausage on legs…

"Doesn't look *that* amazing!" Billy complained, staring at the faint flashing red lights round the collar.

"Yeah, but it shows up in the dark – that's the point, Billy. And it's 11 o'clock in the morning at the moment, if you hadn't noticed. Anyway, are you listening to my story or what?"

Honestly, my mate Billy has the attention span of a *brick*.

"Course!" said Billy indignantly, switching Winslet's collar on and off a few times.

"So, what do you reckon, then? About Keith, I mean?"

Billy shrugged, and began scratching Winslet's ears, which she liked a whole lot more than him mucking about with light switches around her neck.

"Well," he began, after a few seconds' silence, "do you *mumf-mumffy-mumf?*"

"What?"

"I *said*, do you *mumf-mumffy-mumf?*" Billy repeated, while leaning over and ruffling Winslet's ears to the point where her back leg was doing that weird scratching in mid-air thing that dogs do when you hit the right spot.

"Um, are you talking to Winslet or me?" I ask the back of Billy's head.

"You, of course!" he frowned, swivelling his face around in my direction finally.

Before he'd got engrossed in Winslet's Christmas collar, he'd spent most of our conversation staring at the sky, staring at his daft mutt Precious playing with Rolf and Winslet, at faraway rooftops and at his well-chewed nails while I'd been telling him all about Keith and my hot date (OK, lukewarm date).

We tell each other everything, me and Billy – always have, ever since we were too young to even know how to speak properly. Of course, he's never very good at analysing stuff in the way that Sandie is, but sometimes it's quite good to get a boy's take on things, even if – for the most part – I disregard everything he says as being pure drivel. So here we were, doing our usual Sunday morning meet-up/catch-up in the park around Alexandra Palace, and I was sincerely hoping for once that he might say something useful and give me an insight into the workings of Keith Brownlow's mind (i.e. why he felt he had to hit me with a snowball before he plucked up courage to ask me out, and if being stunningly ignorant about computer games was going to ruin my chances of a meaningful relationship).

And instead, all Billy was doing was mumbling incoherently at me.

"Well, if you're speaking to *me*," I told him, "do you fancy talking in English, instead of gibberish?"

Billy started fidgeting with the peak of his baseball cap and coughed a bit. Then he turned his attention back to Winslet, who was irritably clawing at his knee, impatient to have her ears scratched again.

"I just *said*," Billy began again in a louder, but oddly higher voice, "do you fancy him? This Keith lad, I mean…"

"No!" I replied indignantly. "Of course not!"

"Well, why are you seeing him, then? Isn't that the point of dating someone? 'Cause you fancy them?"

Hmm … I'd thought that too.

"But maybe I *will* fancy him, if I get to know him," I said, arguing the point anyway. "And Sandie said it's always good experience."

"Fnar!"

"What's that snort supposed to mean?"

"Well, what's she on about?" Billy frowned (at Winslet, although I knew it was directed at me). "Going out with someone; it's not like it's a job interview or something! It's not something you exactly need 'experience' for, is it? You either like someone or you don't!"

Good *grief*. That was just about the most grown-up thing I'd ever heard Billy come out with. It was almost scary hearing him be so sensible. I think I preferred it when he spoke his usual gibberish…

"Why are you being so stroppy about this? You're as bad as Chloe!"

I'd already told him about Chloe going all frosty on me on Friday, after Keith (via Ben Something-Or-Other) had asked me out. Billy had suggested – in another moment of grown-up sensibleness, I just realized – that maybe Chloe was jealous; not particularly because it was Keith Brownlow doing the asking, but just because it was *me* being asked out and not *her*. Which could make sense, I guess...

"I am *not* as bad as stupid Chloe!" he replied, looking kind of pink around the edges.

God, what was up with him? Billy was normally just this amiable goofball. Had he been replaced with a look-alike alien android? One that was far too sensible and serious for its own good?

"You're not jealous too, are you?" I tried to tease him.

Uh-oh – big mistake.

"Jealous? Huh! Give me a break!" Billy huffed and puffed. "What, just 'cause one lad asks you out, you think *every* lad's going to fancy you?"

"No!" I squeaked, wondering how we'd gone from gentle teasing to major huff in the space of two seconds. What was going on? Me and Billy *always* fooled around and wound each other up – neither of us took offence. Well, never before.

Then much to my surprise (and Winslet's disappointment) Billy stood up, called out to his dog Precious (who ignored him, naturally), and left. Just like that, with only a mumbled "See you..." over his shoulder.

Me and Winslet watched in stunned surprise as he strode off, interrupting his yapping poodle's game of Lick-Chase with Rolf to scoop him up under his arm, and off he went.

"What was that all about, eh, Winnie?" I marvelled, bending down and taking over scratching duties on her furry ears.

Winslet growled low.

"Hey, you little hairy ratbag," I growled back at her. "*You* need to be taught a lesson."

Yes, I know it's cruel, but I'd just remembered we had a pair of foam reindeer antlers in the cupboard at home, left over from last year. As soon as we got back, those antlers were going *straight* on Winslet's head. Let's see how much attitude Miss Growly-knickers had *then*.

And at least in the middle of my sisters' rowing and my friends going weird on me, I might have a laugh and get a little Christmas spirit into the bargain...

Chapter 9

AND THE WINNER IS ... A SHOCK

When it comes to talents, my family's are...
Dad: brilliant at mending bikes.
Grandma: amazing cook.
Linn: great at organizing and picking fights with Rowan.
Rowan: good at arty weird stuff and aggravating Linn.
Tor: all-round animal whisperer.
Me: expert worrier.

Trust me, it's taken years of practice to get as good at worrying as I am. I can worry about all sorts of things: whether we're so poor at the moment that we might have to cancel Christmas; whether my boobs are so small that I might get mistaken for a boy by anyone with poor eyesight; whether Mum's been gone so long she'll forget where we live; whether anyone out there really has X-ray vision and can see me naked through my clothes. Today, I am worried about assembly...

Walking into assembly is usually a painless and dull event. OK, so you know you've got to listen to Mr Bashir witter on about this, that and the other, but he has quite a soothing voice, so we all tend to look at it as a chance to snooze for twenty minutes before the torture that is Monday morning classes starts properly.

But *this* particular Monday, of course, was a different

matter altogether. *This* particular morning I walked into assembly with knees of pure jelly. Somewhere out there amongst the rows and rows of blurred blazers and faces was Keith Brownlow, sitting with his mates. Was he watching me? Were they teasing him? Was he making jokes about our date? On Saturday, had he asked me out again by accident and was he now sitting there regretting it? Oh, the very thought of him looking my way made me so nervous I could *squeak*.

"Eeeppp!"

Sandie turned around sharply at the high-pitched, panicky noise I'd just made in my throat.

"It's OK!" she said reassuringly, knowing exactly how I was feeling. (Funny that, since I'd moaned on to her about how sick I felt every step of the way to school...)

"Eeeppp!" I squeaked again in reply. All I wanted to do was sit down and feel less conspicuous. Then I could relax (a bit).

"Look – I see the others!" Sandie exclaimed, waving over at our friends.

Sure enough: Jen and Kellie appeared to be doing impressions of windmills, they were flapping their arms around so wildly to signal me and Sandie over. As we got to the end of the row of chairs, Salma grinned broadly at us and hauled her and Jen's bags off the two seats they'd been saving. From the far end of the row, Chloe managed a little wave in our direction, but didn't seem to be able to conjure up a smile. Uh-oh – we were still in that mysterious place known as huff-land...

"Where have you been?" Jen said excitedly, widening

her eyes in my direction (very hard to do when you have teeny-tiny button eyes). "We've all been dying to hear about Keith!"

"Yeah, how did it go?" Kellie gushed. "I was going to phone you yesterday but my gran and grandad were visiting..."

"Did you snog him?" Salma grinned wickedly, getting straight to the point.

"Well..." I began, slightly flustered – mainly because Salma's not-very-whispered question had the girls in the row in front turning around to earwig in on the gossip.

Chloe, however, wasn't nearly as interested; oh no – while Salma, Jen, Kellie and the girls in the row in front were just about exploding with curiosity, Chloe was busy rummaging around in her bag, pretending that it was essential that she checked out the contents of her pencil case this very minute.

"Come on, then! Tell! Tell!" Jen urged me.

"Well, I—"

"Quiet down now, boys and girls!" Mr Bashir's booming voice interrupted my what-I-did-at-the-weekend story.

"Boo..." mumbled Salma, as we all shuffled in our chairs under the watchful glare of Mrs Dixon the German teacher, who was on chatter patrol at our side of the hall.

And so assembly got under way with Mr Bashir entertaining us with his usual scintillating selection of topics: "...well done to *blah*, for his excellent *blah* ... must all try harder ... *blah blah*... Year *blah's* upcoming exams *blah blah* … no running in the corridors *blah blah* … Mr *Blah* has reported finding a *blah* in the changing rooms…" Riveting stuff, I can tell you. Or at least it would have been, if I hadn't semi-nodded off.

The thing that made me – and all my friends – wake up very suddenly was Mr Bashir's "And finally…", which this Monday happened to be about the Christmas fashion show.

"And finally," he boomed with a big smile, "I'd like to announce the winning theme for the design section of the upcoming charity fashion show. The theme we've chosen is…"

"Oh, please! Let it be ours!" Sandie whispered beside me.

"…very appropriate for Christmas…"

Drag out the agony, why don't you, Mr Bashir, I thought.

"And that theme is … angels!"

Cue half a row of gasps from me and my friends.

"I'm sure all you would-be designers out there will have *lots* of fun with that," Mr Bashir boomed on enthusiastically. "And the person we have to thank for that inspirational idea is…"

Hold on, I frowned to myself. *Doesn't he mean "people"? There were six of us who came up with it. I might have mentioned angels first, but all five of my mates agreed on it in the end.*

"…Chloe Brennan! Well done, Chloe! Can you come up here on stage, please?"

Cue half a row of girls turning round and watching as

their "friend" stood up grinning and without a backward glance trotted down the aisle to the stage.

"Um...?" muttered Sandie, lost in confusion.

"*Exactly*," I replied, not able to put it any better myself...

Chapter 10

WALKING IN A LOO-ROLL WONDERLAND...

"Oh – an escort home!" grinned Dad, locking up the bike shop and getting a start to see me there waiting for him. "What have I done to deserve this, Ally Pally?"

"Nothing. All I'm going to do is moan," I told him bluntly.

"Moan away," he smiled, lifting my heavy schoolbag off my shoulder and hauling it on to his. "It's in my Parent Contract – it's my job to listen to my children's moans."

My dad, you have to understand, is pretty much perfect. Maybe he could do with being a little less skinny (Grandma's always giving him extra helpings to fatten him up, but he still stays stubbornly lanky), and maybe he's a bit dippy (he mistook Sandie's mobile phone for the TV remote last week and speed-dialled her auntie when he was trying to switch over to *EastEnders*), but apart from that, he's perfect. He's funny, sweet, kind and never gets mad at us – mainly because none of us would ever do anything to make him mad, if we humanly could avoid it. And unlike some of my mates' parents, when it comes to telling him your moans, he'll never laugh at how silly they are or tell you to stop being petty. Even when they *are* silly, petty moans...

"It's about something pretty stupid," I warned him, so he didn't worry that I was about to tell him I was in trouble at school for setting it on fire or anything.

"It's not about the Christmas decorations, is it?" he frowned as we walked through the cold, frosty night towards warm, toasty home. "I know things have been a bit tight, lately, but I've got a couple of bikes getting collected next week so—"

"It's not that, Dad," I stopped him. "Anyway, we all like Rowan's decorations."

It was true – even Linn (who is fair, even if she is a grump) had to admit that Ro's latest effort was very pretty. She'd turned our lavender-painted hall walls into a blizzard, using only loo paper. Before you go thinking that's the worst idea in the world and we were all insane for liking it, let me explain: Rowan had got sheets and sheets of white loo roll, cut them into dainty patterned snowflakes, then randomly Blu-tack'ed them to the walls, starting with only a few at the top and ending up with a whole flurry by the time you got to the skirting board. When you came through the front door – specially if you brought a blast of winter wind in with you – it was just as if you'd walked on to the stage set of *The Snow Queen* or something. I couldn't *wait* to see what she was going to do with the school stage when it came to the fashion show…

Which brought me back to my moan.

"So what's the problem, then?" Dad asked, holding his elbow out for me to link my arm into his.

"I think I've just fallen out with all my friends. Except Sandie."

"Oh. That's not so good. How come?"

How come? 'Cause Chloe had hijacked our idea and taken all the credit, that's how come. And no one but me seemed to think that was a lousy thing to do. (And Sandie, of course, but she always goes along with what I think. Which drives me mad, sometimes.)

All the rest of the way home, I wittered on about how Chloe had gone up on stage, and hadn't even bothered to correct Mr Bashir and tell him we'd *all* come up with the theme together. She just stood there and beamed while he announced that as a prize, she would – of course – get to model in the show. "Of course"? Why "of course"? Shouldn't we all have decided between us who got chosen to model? I know I'd daydreamed that it might be me, at one point, but I'd never have been so presumptuous as to expect it – even if I *had* suggested the angel thing to begin with. If I had to vote I'd have probably gone for Salma, since she's so undeniably gorgeous, looking like a thirteen-year-old version of Penelope Cruz if you catch her from the right angle. Or maybe I'd even have plumped for Sandie, since she's so agonizingly shy and being asked to model would have been a total mind-blowingly amazing thing to happen to her. But what was the point of mulling over all that when Chloe had gone and nominated herself, all because she was the one who'd written up and handed the entry in?

"Well, maybe it's fair enough," Jen had suggested afterwards. "We wouldn't have got around to entering at all if Chloe hadn't done it."

"I know you mentioned angels first, Ally, but Chloe

was the one who wrote the entry out properly," Salma had shrugged.

"Only one of us would have got to model anyway, so it doesn't really matter if Chloe only put her name on the entry and not ours too!" Kellie had reasoned.

And here's the horrible thing; all I cared about was fair play, but the more I tried to argue, the more I sounded like I was suffering from a *serious* case of sour grapes. And that's when my mates swanned off with Chloe, leaving me – and Sandie, I guess – looking like a couple of sulky losers.

"Let the dust settle, Ally," Dad advised me, once I'd bored him to death with all my moaning. "I'm sure that after a night's sleep Chloe will see that she was a little bit out of order. And when they stop to think about it, your other friends will understand that you were trying to stick up for them too, not just for yourself."

I hope so, I thought to myself as I hugged his arm and stared at the welcoming twinkle of the white-fairy-lights-and-pink-feather Christmas wreath on our front door. (The fairy lights, by the way, thankfully turned out to be for outdoor use as well as indoor, as Dad checked after Linn's safety-conscious panic. So we weren't going to go up in a festive bonfire after all.)

"You know something, Ally Pally?" said Dad, opening the front door and letting me into the snowflake-fluttering hall first. "I wouldn't be surprised if one of them phoned you tonight, to say sorry!"

Well, call him a spooky old psychic, but no sooner had we closed the front door (and witnessed a harassed Linn armed with a mountain of paperwork pass a blissed-out Rowan armed with a mountain of junk-shop-find lace curtains and a large pair of scissors), than the phone rang.

"Bet you 10p!" Dad grinned at me, as he hung up his padded denim jacket.

"You're on!" I laughed, rushing to grab the phone off the hall table. "Hello?"

"Wanna come to a Christmas party on Friday?"

So ... Dad *wasn't* a spooky old psychic *and* he owed me 10p. So much for it being one of my buddies phoning up to apologize – it was only Billy. But at least it sounded like old-style Billy, rather than the moody, huffy, alien version I'd met up with yesterday morning.

"Oh, yeah? What sort of party?" I asked warily. Billy's funny and great and everything, but he's not exactly Boy About London, with access to all the hippest party circuits.

"My mum and dad's. Round ours. Should be awful," he explained, selling it to me really appealingly (*not*). "Mum said I could invite a friend, just to stop my head exploding with the sheer corniness and boredom of it all. So I thought of you."

"Gee, you make it sound so tempting!" I grinned down the phone, chuffed to hear the Billy I knew and (didn't quite) love once again, after yesterday morning's blip. "Sure – I'd love to come."

Of course I would. True, it would be – as Billy so rightly put it – both boring and corny, but as I didn't have a better offer for Friday night, then he was on.

"Good. Brilliant. I'm glad. Anyway..."

"Anyway?" I repeated, after a pause from Billy's end of the phone.

"Um ... anyway ... I just wondered: are you still going out with that guy Keith on Wednesday?"

"Might be," I answered him, bristling slightly. "Why?"

"Well, just 'cause I was speaking to some guys in the year above me at school. They play in the school team – against yours. They know *him*. That bloke Keith, I mean."

"*And?*" I demanded irritably. Billy – he was going funny on me again, wasn't he? All defensive and awkward at the mention of Keith Brownlow.

"And ... and well, they said he's a really boring git."

"*Thank* you for that," I said snippily. "I think it's up to *me* to say whether he's boring or not, since *I'm* the one going out with him!"

Billy didn't say anything to that, but in the background I could hear his mum calling him to tea above the sound of Precious's *un*-precious yappity-yapping.

"Uh, see you Friday, then? 'Bout 7.30?"

"Whatever," I mumbled, putting the phone down on him.

What was with my friends today? Was there something going on with the stars? Astrologically-speaking, were all my mates destined to be hopeless at the moment?

"Well?" Dad grinned, peering out from the kitchen doorway at me now. "Was I right?"

"Absolutely!" I grinned back, before adding, "*Not!*"

With a tsk and a roll of his eyes, Dad spun a silver 10p

up in the air in my direction. I held out my hand to catch it, missed completely, and felt it ping off my forehead with a dull painful thunk.

I tell you, Santa had *better* have some excellent surprises up his furry-lined sleeves after all the hassle I was going through at the moment...

Chapter 11

OOF! WHEE! AND BLEE!

"Oof!"

That was me, tripping over a tangle of lace net curtain.

"Sowwy, Awwy!" mumbled Rowan, glancing up from the living-room floor, with her hands clutching yet more net curtain and her mouth dangerously full of pins.

The tangle of lace and pins was the beginnings of Rowan's fledgling angel outfit for next week's fashion show. But at the moment it was more of a health and safety risk than a winning design.

"Maybe you should do that in your room?" I suggested to Ro, looking around at the sewing factory which was once known as our living room.

"Not big enough to spwead out," Rowan said, shaking her head.

I didn't push the point, mainly because I didn't want her to risk talking again and swallow any pins. Anyway, it was Ro's lookout – maybe there *wasn't* enough floor-space in her bedroom to lay out the material and patterns (thanks to her cramming the place full of wall-to-wall spangly clutter) but at least her room had the advantage of a door that could be locked. This room, however, was open house for every furball going, and at the moment Winslet was snoozing and shedding hairs on one spreadeagled curtain, while a cat that wasn't Colin was lazily clawing more lace-like holes on another.

Still, it was her problem – I had important things to do this Tuesday afternoon.

"Bye, bye, Carli and Charlie," I muttered to the photo of my elfin cousins, as I picked it (and the card it had arrived in) up off the mantelpiece.

They were about to be moved to our second division Christmas card display area – the top of the bookshelf on the back wall – now that a VIC (Very Important Card) had arrived.

I heard another "oof!" and turned to see Tor by my side, trying to untangle his foot from a length of netting.

"It's pretty, isn't it?" Tor said for the 56th time since Mum's card had arrived this morning.

"Yep, it's very pretty," I agreed, moving Mum's hand-made sculpturey bits around on the mantelpiece to make room for her large, handmade card.

"Those are lentils," Tor explained to me for the 78th time, pointing to the metallic card.

"I know," I smiled at him, trying not to sound irritated.

After all, he was excited, and after all, it must have taken Mum an eternity to stick on all those dried lentils before she spray-painted the whole thing silver. In the middle, the lentils spelt out "Happy Christmas!" in swirly, Victorian-type letters, and all around the letters were snowflakes and snowmen and robins and Christmas crackers – all "drawn" in lentils. On the left-hand side was something that looked like a rabbit, which confused us all at first (what did rabbits have to do with Christmas?) – until we realized it was supposed to be a reindeer.

"'*For Linn, Rowan, Ally and Tor, with dollops of love, big fat kisses and squishy hugs for Christmas and for ever – Mum xxxxx*'." Tor flipped open the card and read aloud for the 33rd time. "'*P.S. And save one of those kisses for Dad!*' Where did this card come from again, Ally?"

"The postmark was from Ghana – remember?" I told him for the trillionth, zillionth time. He'd even helped me find Ghana on the huge map I have on the wall of my room upstairs, where I track all our globetrotting mother's movements. I'd even let him put the coloured pin in to show her latest destination.

"Oh, yes…" Tor nodded slowly, closing the card with the greatest delicacy, as if it was highly fragile and valuable. All the same, a couple of lentils fell off (the envelope had been full of them).

"Right," I muttered, turning and tiptoeing across the living-room floor, landing on each patch of lace-free carpet or wood floor like they were stepping stones. "There you go, Carli and Charlie! I hope you'll be very happy!"

As I manoeuvred a few cards to make space for the twins, I caught sight of a couple of envelopes tucked at the back – the sort of envelopes that have those little business-type windows in them, with scaryish red writing glaring out. Hmm … since me and my sisters and brother are all officially "kids", Dad doesn't like to bother us with the detail of bills and how much trouble he has paying them sometimes, but I think even Tor is smart enough to know that business-type letters with red writing mean money is tight.

Speaking of Tor...

"Ally."

"Yep?" I said, turning around and finding him magically by my side again, having followed my stepping-stone path past Rowan's masterpiece.

"Secret Santa," he said earnestly.

"Secret Santa," I repeated. I knew what Secret Santa was; we did that a couple of times at primary school. Everybody pulls someone's name out of a hat, and secretly buys them a present. Then on the day the presents are all handed out, everyone gets one, but no one knows who from. It's kind of fun.

"His class are doing it this year," Rowan filled me in, having thankfully taken the pins out of her mouth and shoved them in the fabric on the floor. "He wants some-one to help him choose a present to buy. He already asked me, but I've got to make this angel outfit and do the set design stuff too."

"What about Linn?"

"She's too busy bossing everyone about and drawing up battle plans for the fashion show..." Ro muttered dryly.

"Will you help me, Ally?"

"No problem!" I told our brother. And why not? Everyone else was so busy doing important things round our house that as the sister currently doing nothing more important than twiddling her thumbs, of *course* I could help him out. "Who have you got to buy a present for?"

"Ella," Tor replied, mentioning the name of a classmate I hadn't heard him talk about before. Well, for Ella's sake, I was glad to help – left to his own devices, Tor would probably end up getting her a bird-seed dispenser or a novelty squeaky dog toy or something.

"You know, maybe *we* should all do a Secret Santa this year, instead of buying each other presents..." I thought out loud, musing over how much money that would save our family. I mean, it wasn't just Dad buying *us* lot a present each – it was the fact that he might not be able to dole out extra gift-buying pocket money, beyond what he normally gave us. If I just had to buy *one* thing for *one* person in the family, I wouldn't need any extra cash at all. And if I didn't have to buy pressies for my former friends (oh, yes – Chloe and everyone were most *definitely* giving me and Sandie the cold shoulder today), then it *could* be the most cost-saving Christmas I'd ever had...

"See? Every cloud has a silver lining, Ally," I could practically hear my grandma's voice reassuring me, over the fall-out with my mates.

"That's a very good idea, Ally!" is what Grandma *actually* said, as she busily bustled into the living room with a can of Pledge and a duster in her hands. "I think that could be a lot of fun, if we all did that this year! Don't you, Rowan? Don't you, Tor?"

Detective Inspector Ally Love here at your service; and if I wasn't very much mistaken, Grandma was acting *very* suspiciously indeed there. It's just that she's just about the *least* excitable person in the entire universe. (A freak tornado could rain showers of frogs down from the sky and all she'd do is tsk and put her umbrella up.) Something told me that her enthusiasm hid the fact that she was in on exactly *how* poor we were right now...

"Hellooo! Wait till you see what *I've* got!" came a holler, followed by a clatter at the front door, and some insane barking.

Tor darted out into the hallway to see what Dad was hollering and clattering about, and what exactly Rolf was barking at. It had to be *something* good, from the happy "Wow!" we heard Tor shout out next. Two seconds and some rustling later, me, Rowan and Grandma were let in on the surprise.

"Ta na!" Dad grinned in the living room doorway, as he presented the wonkiest, most lopsided Christmas tree I'd ever seen. It had gaps where branches should be, looked like it had shed half its pine needles already and was bent over at the top. It matched our house perfectly. I loved it.

"Wheeee!" Tor's face peered through a gap in the greenery. At his feet, a panting Rolf limbo-danced under the bottom-most branches, then stood up straight, shaking himself madly and sending loose pine needles flying.

"I got it for free, from the flower shop down the road," Dad explained, taking broad strides over Rowan's handiwork to temporarily prop up the tree by the fireplace. "I did a swap – said I'd fix the brakes on the owner's bike in exchange."

"Well done, Martin!" Grandma enthused some more, which translated as "Well, done for saving more money!", obviously...

"I'll make some baubles for it, when I've got a minute!" Rowan offered. "I'll get more pine cones at the weekend."

And not leave them in the same room as Rolf, unattended, I thought.

"But we need an angel!" Tor suddenly frowned up at the lopsided top of the tree.

Ah, yes, something was still missing.

"Rolf!" Grandma burst out.

At first I was going to tell her that it didn't seem such a good idea – Rolf weighed too much and would break several branches if you tried to balance him up there – and *then* I saw what she meant...

Our charming dog, who had been working all our nerves badly recently with his irritating habits, had just added one *more* irritating habit to his repertoire.

"Did he just *pee* on that?" I asked, aghast, as Rolf lowered his cocked leg from the tree.

No one needed to answer my question. From the rapidly spreading puddle on the living room floor, the answer was most definitely *yes*.

Blee...!

Chapter 12

DULL DATES AND SACKED SISTERS

"It must be *so* flattering to be asked out by a boy!" Sandie sighed wistfully, her lips only *just* visible above the top of her wound-around stripy scarf.

"Yeah, I guess so," I nodded, half-wishing Keith Brownlow would hurry up (it was so nose-freezingly cold standing here waiting for him this Wednesday afternoon), and half-hoping he wouldn't show up at all. I mean, the flattery side was great in theory, but I had two problems here: a) I could seriously do without this so-nervous-I-could-barf sensation – if this was what love felt like, I wasn't sure if I liked it, and b) I wasn't sure if I *liked* Keith, never mind *fancied* him or even *loved* him. I'd only hung out with him for five minutes. He hit me with a snowball once, for God's sake. And it was kind of hard to concentrate on this date when I had other stuff on my mind, like the fact that Chloe and everyone had just come out of school, taken one look at me and Sandie waiting by the main gate, and immediately detoured to the side gate instead. Good grief – were we poisonous or something…?

"Here he comes, here he comes, here he comes!" Sandie gushed, thankfully not too loudly (her words were muffled by her scarf).

Urgh, there went my stomach, doing a front roll followed by a back flip at the sight of Keith lurching towards me, hunched up in his blazer against the biting cold.

"He's so cute!" Sandie whispered.

Was he? I narrowed my eyes and tried to take a good look at him, without sheer panic clouding my vision. Before, when I just knew him as some older guy at school, I'd have described him as tallish, OK-looking-ish with brown spikyish hair. Now that I was almost kind of going out with him, I'd describe him ... exactly the same. He was just a bit "ish", really. Today, I should really make the effort to get to know and like him better, or as Billy had said, there wasn't much point in dating him.

"Hi..." mumbled Keith, in a friendlyish way.

"Hi..." I mumbled back, in a shyish way. "Um, this is my friend Sandie."

"Yeah, I know," shrugged Keith, giving Sandie a small nod of recognition.

I could feel the hot beam of happiness radiating off Sandie as he said that. An older boy knew who she was? That was about the most exciting thing that had happened to her since she caught sight of some bloke who used to be in, *EastEnders* at the cheese counter of our local supermarket. (He bought some Mature Cheddar. She knew for a fact because she stalked him for about quarter of an hour.)

"Fancy the park?" Keith asked me, his hands wedged deep in his pockets and his elbows bobbing back and forth awkwardly while he talked.

"The park at Ally Pally or Priory Park?" I checked with him, as I tried to hide my disappointment. What I *really* wanted to do was hang out in a café – any café, as long as it had a radiator I could attach my shivery self to.

"Just Ally Pally," he said, nodding his head over in the direction of the broad iron gates across the road that led to the Palace's car parks.

And then he started walking. It took a split-second for me to work out that I was meant to follow him, and then another split-second to realize that Sandie *wasn't* meant to be coming with us. I turned and threw her a wide-eyed look that said "Where are *you* going?"

"Oh! Oh, right!" Sandie blushed, suddenly realizing that she should be *anywhere* but on my date with me. "Bye, then!"

A set of traffic lights, a mostly silent stroll into the park, a stilted chat about which teachers we liked and which teachers we didn't, and I started to relax a tiny bit.

But when Keith started to rant on endlessly about computer games again ("Can't stay long! Got to get to Wood Green and pick up the new *Mega Sega Master Blaster Brain Melt* game*. Have you played that yet?"), I started to wish Sandie had stuck with us. At least I could have had a decent conversation while Keith talked to himself, which is practically what he was doing now, since he didn't let me get a word in edgeways.

* I might have made that one up. Couldn't remember what the stupid game was *really* called … my own brain had melted when he was describing all the levels he'd got to in graphic, mind-frying detail…

But my stunning lack of knowledge when it came to computer games *didn't* seem to put Keith Brownlow off. *Or* the fact that I spent the last few minutes of our conversation babbling about how we couldn't get the smell of wee out of our Christmas tree thanks to Rolf peeing on it. (Well, I panicked – it was the first thing I thought of when he paused long enough to let me speak.)

Oh no – Keith Brownlow wasn't put off; quite the opposite. In fact, he'd (eek!) even asked me out again. On Saturday night, me and Keith were going for a pizza. Maybe it would be a case of third time lucky; maybe sitting down with him (instead of strolling and getting frostbite with him) would help me get to know him better; maybe he'd even (double eek!) try and *kiss* me...

I was still so bewildered (did I like him?) and in shock (about being asked out again), that when I got back home, I thought for a second that I was in the wrong house. I didn't have a clue who the girl in the kitchen was, with loose wavy fair hair tumbling around her face. Then she glanced up at me and I realized it was Linn in disguise.

"What are you doing?" I asked her, as she turned her attention back to the reams of scribbled-on paper that were taking up every square centimetre of our big table.

Over by the cooker, Grandma was stirring something fantastic-smelling, while looking over disapprovingly at Linn's mess, which was going to have to get cleared soon before we could all eat.

"I'm trying to stress myself to death," Linn said flatly.

Actually, you could see that she *was* stressed; apart

from not bothering to blow-dry her hair poker-straight (unheard of), I saw that her face was wiped-out white and she had these pink blobs of panic on her cheeks.

"Is the fashion show really complicated to sort out, then?" I asked, noticing Rolf under the table, chewing on something that looked suspiciously like one of Linn's pristine highlighter pens. Bending down as though I was getting something out of my bag while I talked, I distracted Rolf with a pat on the head, then just as he started panting with happiness, I yanked the crumpled yellow highlighter out of his mouth.

"It's *horribly* complicated to sort out," Linn sighed, dropping her head in her hands.

Great – that gave me a second to wipe the saliva off the pen and shove it back on the table before she noticed it was gone. In the mood she was in, Rolf, really, *really* didn't want to antagonize her.

"She's just had to sack Rowan," Grandma explained in a low voice, as though that would cause less grief. It didn't – Linn just dropped her head further down on to her crossed arms, rustling papers as she did so.

"Sack her?" I bleated, confused. *Could* you actually sack someone from being a sister?

"Her ideas for the set design were too … extreme," Grandma explained to me. "They were going to cost too much and take too long to do."

Aha – so Ro was sacked from the *fashion* show, not our *family*…

"I *told* her she couldn't have real ice on the stage – not with all the electrics!" I heard Linn muttering to herself.

"Apparently, Rowan wanted to hire a dry ice machine and a snow-blower," Grandma chipped in, raising her eyes to the ceiling.

"Never mind the huskies..." mumbled Linn.

"Huskies?" I looked at Grandma in alarm.

"One of the other girls on the committee caught Rowan putting signs up around school asking for anyone with huskies to audition them for the show," she drawled. "So the committee decided Rowan should go, before everything got out of hand. And they asked Linn to do it, since she's her sister."

"Where's Ro now?" I asked. As if I needed to. It didn't take much to picture her sobbing in her pillow.

"In her room sticking pins in a wax figure of me, I think." Linn managed a wry smile as she lifted her head off the table. "God, Ally, count yourself lucky that you aren't involved in this stupid show..."

I shot a glance at Grandma, who knew – since I'd moaned to her about the situation with Chloe and everyone – how disappointed I was *not* to be. But listening to Linn right now was changing my mind fast; there seemed to be nothing very glamorous about mounds of paper and stress.

"Could you go and have a word with Rowan, Ally?" Grandma asked, looking over at me. "You know you can always calm her down."

Course I'd speak to her. After all, Rowan had been sacked from the fashion show and I'd been sacked by most of my friends. We had loads in common...

Chapter 13

JINGLE BALLS

It's very odd when people you used to gossip with all the time stop talking to you altogether. Or *looking* at you even. In every single class we were in together, Chloe, Kellie, Salma and Jen were doing this amazing job of staring straight through me and Sandie, as if we didn't exist. It was pretty upsetting, really. *And* unfair...

"This?"

Tor had interrupted my gloomy thoughts by running over to me and holding up a small book called *All You Need To Know About Earthworms*. Thank goodness for small, animal-obsessed brothers when you're in a bad mood. If it hadn't been for Tor and his Secret Santa shopathon this Thursday afternoon, I'd probably just have spent a sorry-for-myself hour or five staring out of my bedroom window. This was the fourth day of Chloe's and the girls' silent treatment at school and it was definitely starting to get me down.

("Maybe you should go up to them, ask them straight out what's going on!" Sandie suggested at breaktime this morning. "Or phone one of them at home maybe!" Maybe ... and then again maybe not. I had my pride and didn't see why I should have to do the grovelling when I hadn't done anything wrong. Unlike Chloe...)

"No, Tor – I don't think Ella will like that," I said, shaking my head at the earthworm book. "How about you get her this pencil set, with Sabrina the Teenage Witch on it?"

Tor scrunched his nose up, but seemed to see sense. Teenage witches might seem pretty dull to him – compared to the never-ending joy of worms – but I think he was anxious to start searching out our second purchase of the day.

Two minutes after queuing to pay for the pencils in WH Smith, we were on the escalator that would lead us to the first floor of the shopping centre and the wonderland of Woolworths' Christmas decorations department. Grandma – in a bid to cheer Tor up (he was still gutted to be Joseph and not a sheep in his nativity play) – had given us a fiver to go and buy a new angel for, as we now all knew it, the wee tree. (And it wasn't called that just because it was small...)

"Come on, then! Race you to the angels!" I laughed, scooting off in the direction of Woollies and leaving him behind.

With a determined grin, he shot past me at high speed, his short legs carrying him into the shop and off in search of twinkly bits while I bounded slower, realizing I might be coming over like a teenage shoplifter making my escape to the suspicious-looking security guard strutting around.

"Look!" Tor grinned, when I finally caught up with him. "Rowan!"

He was holding up a dark-haired doll in a doily, with

cardboard wings stapled on to her back. It did look a *tiny* bit like Rowan, who was, incidentally, surprisingly dry-eyed when I went up to her room yesterday, after her barney with Linn. Instead of sobbing into her rose-patterned pillow, Rowan was sitting on her bed, feverishly stitching her angel outfit – absolutely determined to enter the design-a-costume part of the fashion show now that she'd been chucked off the set side of things.

"Not right for our tree, though, is it?" I scrunched my nose up at Tor, putting the mass-produced angel back in the rack beside all the identical versions of her. After Mum's fat Fimo angel, it was going to be very hard to find something that would match up.

"S'pose." Tor shrugged.

"Hey, like my new earrings?" I grinned at him, grabbing two silver baubles up and holding one at each ear. "*Jingle Balls, Jingle Balls...*"

We'd just started singing our terrible Christmas pun of a song when I stopped dead – at the sight of Chloe, Kellie, Jen and Salma over by the giant boxes of every kind of chocolate on the shelves. They were all chatting and laughing, but I could have sworn that Kellie – who was facing our direction – had clocked me.

"Duck!" I whispered in alarm to Tor, who immediately carried on standing exactly where he was.

"Why are you hiding?" he stared down at me (and the dangling silver balls still wound round my ears).

"Because I've just seen Chloe and my other friends and they're not talking to me."

"But if they're not talking to you, why are you

bothering to hide?" said Tor, making a lot of sense for a seven year old who thought a book about earthworms would make a good Secret Santa present.

"It's complicated," I tried to explain, which was hard to do convincingly since I was hunched down in the middle of Woolworths picking up dust on my knees, with Christmas decorations dangling from either side of my head.

"Doesn't matter. They're going now," Tor shrugged. "Well, all of them except Kellie."

"And where is she?" I asked my personal top spy.

"There," said Tor, turning his gaze and pointing to a spot somewhere behind me. About ten centimetres behind me, as it turned out.

"Ally?"

"Uh-huh?" I muttered, trying to rise to my feet as casually as I could, while struggling to slip the baubles off my ears.

Kellie smiled nervously, then threw a glance over her shoulder as if she was looking for something. Or someone.

I saw Tor gaze at me, then at Kellie, then back again, wondering what exactly was going on with us and our non-speaking policy. Much like I was.

"Listen, Ally – I'm really sorry about … stuff," Kellie burbled speedily, her black eyebrows arching up into peaks as she apologized. "I wish we hadn't fallen out."

"Me too," I nodded with relief. "But I didn't want to fall out, Kel – and I didn't mean for this to be some big fight between us. I just didn't think it was fair for Chloe to take all the credit for our idea, that was all!"

"I know," Kellie shrugged sheepishly.

Hmm. Well, if she knew, why hadn't she or any of my other friends spoken to me for four days? Before I could ask her that very question, she started talking again.

"Look, it was just that Chloe asked us all to choose sides – hers or yours! And you know what Chloe can be like!"

And suddenly I understood – strong-willed, confident Chloe, or wimpy, wittery Ally. No wonder the other girls found themselves rail-roaded into backing Chloe. But that still didn't solve the mystery of why Chloe had taken such a moody on me...

"But Kel—" I began, only to have her interrupt me straight away.

"Look, I'd better go and catch the others up – I pretended I had to buy something for my mum so I could have an excuse to sneak over and talk to you."

"Um, OK," I shrugged, feeling kind of funny that she was taking off again so soon.

"Hey, we're still mates, OK?" Kellie smiled sadly at me as she started backing away. "But in secret. Yeah?"

"Ally..." said Tor, once we'd watched Kellie scurry out of the doors and off along the shopping concourse.

"Yep?"

"How do you be friends 'in secret'?" he blinked up at me.

"Tor," I muttered, totally bemused, "I have absolutely *no* idea..."

Chapter 14

LINN'S "LOVELY" SURPRISE

"Biscuits! Yay!"

I know I must have sounded to Linn like an over-excited kindergarten kid when I caught sight of the small biscuit tin on the table, but the very thought of a sugar hit was just about bliss after the day *I'd* just had. Boredom? There'd been plenty of that (thanks to dull lessons). Weirdness? Yep, I'd had that too (thanks to more blanking by my "friends", secret or otherwise).

"Whoah!" said Linn, glancing up from her endless, diagram-doodled sheets of paper. "Read that first before you start cheering..."

She passed me a note, which I thought was more of her fashion show scribblings, till I focused in and recognized Grandma's handwriting.

"Where is she?" I asked, glancing around. Our gran comes and makes our tea and eats with us every week-night. I sure could smell something good wafting out of the oven, but there was no sign of Grandma – Tor had been doing his homework by himself in the living room when I stuck my head around the door three seconds ago.

"She's feeling bad, so she's gone home," Linn told me. "Flu, she thinks – she didn't want to hang around and spread her germs around to us."

"Oh," I frowned, not used to our ever-capable and resilient gran having anything wrong with her. (Getting bugs and germs and sniffles was *our* job.)

"*Dear All*,'" I began mumbling her note out aloud. "*Sorry to disappoint you, but the tin is a biscuit-free zone (it came from my house, and I'm afraid me and my neighbour Nancy made short work of the shortbread that used to be in it.) Instead, it's full of bits of paper with all our names scribbled on for the Secret Santa. Please pick one and KEEP IT SECRET!*' Why's she said that? We're not dumb! That's why it's called Secret Santa, isn't it?"

"It's probably for Rowan's sake," Linn grinned. "You know what an airhead she is…"

Well, no one could argue with that.

But Grandma's note wasn't quite finished.

"*As we all agreed, no one should spend more than £5 on their present*'," I continued to mumble aloud. "*Oh, and by the way, Ally, your sisters are both really busy with their fashion show bits and pieces, so could you take over from me this weekend and coach your brother on his part for the Nativity? He keeps baaing every time I try to get him to practise Joseph's lines…*'"

Uh-oh, and his school play was only a week away. Unless Tor could convince an audience that Joseph spoke in the ancient biblical language of "baa", we had a problem.

"Hey, Ally, I've got a surprise for you…" said Linn ominously, leaning back on the kitchen chair.

I wasn't sure if I liked Linn having a surprise for me. If it was Tor, the surprise might have been a drawing of his favourite mouse (i.e. a blob with a tail); if it was a surprise from Rowan, it could be something like a handmade brooch she'd done for me (i.e. a blob with some sequins stuck on it). But *Linn* having a surprise for me sounded like trouble, as if she was going to direct me to a cupboard that needed cleaning or tell me that she was going to give me extra tutoring in maths because my marks were always so lousy.

"Oh?" I squeaked, trying not to sound worried.

"Yeah," Linn smiled (hadn't seen that for a while, with her being so busy and stressed and growly lately). "I've wangled it for you to help out at the fashion show!"

"Oh!" I repeated in a slightly different tone of voice. I wasn't actually sure if that was such a good idea – after all, there was someone modelling in the blimmin' fashion show that I didn't exactly want to be in close proximity to. And that was one little non-angel called Chloe Brennan...

"Well, you could try and be a bit more excited, Ally!" Linn frowned, her smile slipping from her face. "I did this as a favour, you know! Grandma told me you were really disappointed not to be involved!"

Well, yeah, I *had* been, but now I didn't think it was such a great idea at all. But surprises and favours from Linn are thin on the ground, so I guessed I should try and look a little more thrilled than I actually felt.

"No! It's great! It really is!" I babbled.

Linn broke into a huge warm smile – it was bedazzling. It made my lie and the stupid fake grin I'd slapped on my face worthwhile. And then I realized that unless there was something seriously wrong with her eyes, she wasn't actually looking at *me*...

"Hi, Alfie! Where did you come from? I didn't hear the doorbell!" she beamed.

I turned slowly, feeling the beads of sweat break out on my forehead as I gazed at his gorgeousness.

"Yeah ... well, Tor was looking out the window as I came up the path, so he let me in," Alfie shrugged casually, leaning on the door frame like the star of some hip art-house movie in his beat-up long suede jacket and spiky blond hair. (And those cheekbones, those cheekbones...)

"Rolf! Leave!" Linn suddenly snapped, spotting Rolf settle down to chew the laces on Alfie's trainers.

"No problem," said Alfie, with a typically casual jolt of his pretty head. "So what are you guys up to?"

"Not much," Linn replied. "Ally's just offered to help me out at next week's fashion show. Haven't you, Al?"

"Nyunghhh," I heard a dorky voice that belonged to me answer. (Why does that *always* happen when Alfie's within earshot? It's not fair! It's like I'm allergic to him or something!)

"You still coming to see it?" Linn asked him, ignoring my grunt.

"Yeah ... sure..." He nodded at Linn, and then – shock horror – at me.

And there, in that one tiny look, I decided that Chloe couldn't scare me if she ran up to me at the fashion show with a man-eating sabre-toothed tiger for company. Of *course* I'd help out, if Alfie was going to be there on the night...

Chapter 15

BAD BREATH, BAD JOKES

"So, Billy, *ha, ha, ha…*"

Uh-oh. I knew what was coming next.

"Is this – *ha, ha, ha* – your girlfriend, then?" asked the smug middle-aged man with the worst bad breath I'd ever encountered.

"Um, no," Billy shook his head, staring at me up and down. "I've never seen her before in my life. She's a gatecrasher, I think. Quick, call the police!"

Mr Bad Breath frowned, then made this unfunny-sounding guffaw, then ambled off to talk to the "grown-ups" and eat more of the nibbly, cheesy, garlicky things Billy's mum was proudly passing around on a tray, just so his breath could be *that* bit more gruesome for the next person who was unfortunate enough to talk to him.

"Nice try at a joke," I complimented my mate.

"Pity that guy was too thick to get it," said Billy, gazing off from the sofa we were sitting on towards the sea of slightly squiffy, slightly obnoxious guests at his parents' Christmas party.

"But hey," I said. "You know something?"

"What?" asked Billy, before taking a slug of his Coke.

"If *one* more person here tonight asks me if I'm your

girlfriend I'm going to kill them. Or you. Or myself. I don't care which," I told him.

I know I'd thought it might be fun (in a twisted way) to come to this party, but I really would have had more fun staying at home and watching Rolf eat the contents of our beanbag (his latest annoying habit). Even counting the hundreds of polystyrene balls he left spread on the floor would be better than sitting here with Billy and being patronized by strangers.

I mean ... Billy being my boyfriend – the very idea!

"Twiglet?" Billy grinned apologetically, hoping he could woo me out of my bad mood with food. As if! It would take more than a Twiglet to make me smile. (A bowl of nachos might have helped, of course.)

"No thanks." I shook my head. "So where's Precious tonight?"

"In my room, out of the way. Mum thought he might get a bit excitable with so many people here."

Translation: "Precious might yap so much someone could be tempted to Sellotape his jaws shut."

"Why don't we go and keep him company?" I suggested. And trust me, it isn't often (in fact, it isn't *ever*) that I'd voluntarily offer to spend time in close proximity to Precious. Normally, I'd rather go for unnecessary fillings at the dentist than spend any time in close proximity to Precious. That dog's main hobby is licking its bum, and I can tell you now that that's *no* fun to watch...

"Yeah, I guess we *could* go to my room. But Mum might be a bit funny about that."

"How come?" I quizzed him.

"All her and dad's friends and the neighbours. I think they might think it's a bit … y'know … me having a girl in my room and everything."

I watched him squirm and wondered what he was on about.

"Billy, I go to your room all the time, normally. I always have, ever since we were about two years old."

"Yeah, I know, but before the party started, Mum said to me that we shouldn't go up to my room while people were here. Just in case it looked a bit … *funny*. With us being teenagers and everything. And you being a girl and me being a—"

"Moron," I said, finishing the sentence for him. "Look, Billy, what's the problem? Don't they understand? You're just my mate. It's not like you're my boyfriend or anything!"

"Of course –" Billy gave me a sarky look – "you've got one of those already!"

How irritating. He'd managed to make me blush, for goodness' sake. Now if anyone was looking, they would probably think we *were* going out, and I was just acting all girlish and shy.

"So … still going out with boring old Keith tomorrow night?" Billy asked, while I was spluttering around for a smart answer to his last comment.

"*Yes*, I'm going out with him!" I managed to say, although I couldn't bring myself to say he wasn't boring. Since I wasn't exactly convinced of that fact myself so far.

"Kissed him, yet?" my cheeky monkey of a mate dared to ask next.

"*No!*" I replied, my eyes wide with stunned surprise at his nerve.

"Well – *ha, ha, ha...*" he sniggered, sounding horribly like Mr Bad Breath for a second there. "If you need someone to practise on, I could maybe help you out – as a friend, of course!"

I checked out Billy's usually dopey but cute face for signs of fever or madness but couldn't see anything obvious.

"OK, I'm going to get the bus home now..." I muttered, pushing myself off the sofa and making a beeline for the hallway and my coat.

"Ally! It was only a joke! Honest!" I heard Billy call after me. A joke? That was about as funny as Rolf eating the beanbag and being sick on Dad's bed as a result.

What *also* wasn't funny was the couple standing nearest to us, sniggering and saying, "Lovers' tiff!" in our direction.

"Ally! I'm sorry! Please!"

I didn't forgive Billy.

However I *did* let him walk me to the bus stop. With a Twiglet up each nostril and one sticking out each ear as punishment.

Firm but fair, I think you'll agree...

Chapter 16

THE UNDRESSED REHEARSAL

How could I *not* have wanted to help out at the fashion show? Apart from the thrill of knowing Alfie was going to be there on the night, this first rehearsal I'd turned up for was *amazing* entertainment. And so far, all I'd had to do was sit in the darkened auditorium with my mouth hanging open at the disaster unfolding in front of me. It was a bit like watching an episode of *ER*, where there's mayhem and madness going on everywhere, and just as you think it can't get any worse, it *does*...

"Hold on, hold on, hold *on*! Stop right there!"

A distorted version of Travis's old hit "Why Does It Always Rain On Me?" squealed to an ungainly halt, as did the line of sulky-looking girls wandering about on stage in jeans and fleeces. It was Saturday afternoon, it was the dress rehearsal for next Wednesday's fashion show, and everything was going really, really smoothly.

Ho, ho, ho, as Santa in a sarcastic mood might say.

The person yelling for everyone to stop was Miss Sylvester from the Design and Tech department, who had been volunteered by Mr Bashir to oversee this whole thing. By her side was my sister Linn, clutching a clipboard so hard that I could practically see how white her knuckles were from where I was sitting. And no wonder her knuckles were white; for a dress rehearsal, there certainly weren't many dresses, or any *other* clothes being shown off, apart from what the "models" themselves had turned up in. And as for a backdrop – well, there wasn't one. Maybe Rowan's ideas for the set design were too stupidly bizarre, but it didn't look like the rest of the team she'd left behind had done much of anything. Or maybe they were just going for the minimal look, i.e. a totally bare stage...

"Gus!" Miss Sylvester yelled over her shoulder into the darkness. "What the hell is going on with this music! It sounds like Travis are playing underwater!"

"Sorry!" a disembodied voice called out from somewhere I couldn't see. "Something's happened to the deck – I think it's... Oh, hold on. It just chewed up the tape!"

"Great!" Miss Sylvester sighed theatrically, while I watched Linn scribble something frantically on her clipboard. (Probably "HELP!!!")

On stage, the "models" (Shakira, Estelle and Linn's mate Mary, all from Sixth Form) stood chewing gum with their hands on their hips.

"OK, girls," Miss Sylvester turned to them next. "I know it's hard to do this when the music's out of synch and the coats you're supposed to be wearing haven't turned up yet, but is there any chance you could try that again, with a little more *enthusiasm* this time?"

"We *were* enthusiastic, Miss!" Mary bleated from the stage.

"Not from here you weren't. You looked bored. And what exactly was with that walk you were doing, Shakira?"

Shakira's walk *had* been pretty weird to watch. She was swaggering and swaying so much that she looked like she was struggling to walk along the deck of a boat being buffeted about in a Force 10 gale.

"It's attitude, Miss," Shakira shrugged. "All the best models have attitude."

"Well, from down here it looks more like you're lolloping about because someone's just shot you with a tranquillizer dart. Now, how about we get a bit more life into this, girls! Let's try this one more time – *without* music. I'll count you through it. And everyone involved in the angels section, can you gather down here please, so we can have a chat before you do your run-through!"

And so Miss Sylvester started clapping, while Shakira, Estelle and Mary bumbled through their steps with even less enthusiasm than before. In the meantime, a flurry of angels drifted down from the side of the stage or through the main doors, and slipped into the front row or generally huddled near Miss Sylvester and Linn. There were tall angels and short angels, traditional (girl) angels and a Barbie-style glitter angel (Jason Bryant, doing his bit for equal rights), convincing angels, and angels that looked more like Romans in togas, or clothes driers with a bunch of sheets slung over them.

But my eyes automatically zoomed in on two angels in particular – my sister Rowan, and Chloe....

Right at that second, Rowan was being hauled to one side by Linn and, from their body language, I could tell straight away they were having a whispered argument. I knew what it was about: Rowan was the only "angel" who hadn't turned up in costume today. ("I want it to be a surprise on the night!" she'd beamed at me over a late breakfast this morning, *long* after early-bird Linn had already set off to rehearsals.) This was obviously just one more aggravating factor in Linn's long, *long* scribbled list of aggravations to do with today's rehearsal.

Chloe, meanwhile, was sitting directly in front of me, five rows down. I could see she was wearing something white (natch), but I couldn't make out the details of it. As the winner of the theme competition, she was going to lead all the girls (and Jason) on stage, wearing something that Miss Sylvester had run up.

I tapped what was left of my bitten nails on the seat beside me, and stared hard at the back of Chloe's head, trying to laser my way beneath the red hair and figure out what was going on in that brain of hers. But as I have no magical powers (more's the pity), I decided that the only way I could get to the bottom of what was going on with her was to – gulp – *ask*.

So, with shaky legs, I got up and padded down the aisle towards her, trying to convince myself that she wasn't *that* scary.

Yeah, *right*...

"Chloe?" I mumbled, staring down at her.

Chloe glanced up, dead-eyed. She actually *did* look kind of scary, but not in the way I expected: all the white material of the dress against her milk white skin; she could have been auditioning for the lead role in a remake of *Caspar the Friendly Ghost*...

"OK, enough!" Miss Sylvester suddenly roared at the

stage, shooing away Shakira, Estelle and Mary. "Angels? can you gather round me, please?"

Without uttering a word to me, Chloe stood up and strode off, lifting her long skirt up just high enough for me to see the dirty trainers she was wearing underneath. One of her wire-framed wings was bent over and flopping, I noticed, with a certain amount of satisfaction.

But I didn't get long to gloat; while Miss Sylvester doled out catwalk tips to the gaggle of angels, Linn spotted me and came scurrying over.

"Come on, Ally! We need to get *you* sorted now!"

"Doing what?" I frowned at her. "There's no audience yet!"

Y'know, when Linn told me what exactly I'd be doing at the fashion show, I had wondered what was the point of me turning up to this rehearsal today in the first place. I mean, showing people to their seats – it's not exactly brain surgery, is it? The seats weren't even going to be numbered, for goodness' sake. My job was just to pack them in and get everyone to move up, so there were no gaps and plenty of seats for everyone. Glamorous, huh?

"Ally, just 'cause there's no audience doesn't mean you shouldn't practise your part!" Linn said in the sort of disappointed, must-try-harder voice I'm more used to hearing from one of my teachers, when my test results are less than fantastic.

"But how am I supposed to do that?" I asked her, gazing around at the rows and rows of empty seats in the auditorium.

"Act it out!"

"What?"

"Act it out! Go over to the door, then pretend you're leading people to their seats!"

I stared at Linn, trying to figure out whether she was joking or not. From the look on her face, the answer was "not".

"I can't do that!" I burbled, feeling my toes curl in embarrassment already.

"Ally – just do it. I'm having enough hassles today, and I don't need another of my sisters making my job more difficult..."

And with that piece of emotional blackmail ringing in my ears, I reluctantly dragged myself over to the main hall door, and starting *miming* showing people in. How embarrassing is *that*?

I couldn't believe Linn had actually persuaded me to do this, especially when I glanced up at the stage – right when I was wafting my arm around, ushering an invisible no one to their seat – and saw Chloe Brennan smirking down at me.

Smirking! Oh, the shame...

THE DIFFERENCE BETWEEN "OOH" AND "AHH"

Sandie's polo-neck jumper didn't like me much – it was trying to strangle me.

It was a gorgeous shade of powder blue, and nice and fitted, but kind of *too* fitted around the neck, if you see what I mean. Or maybe I just had a really thick neck. Whatever, I kept fidgeting with it, trying to loosen it so that talking and swallowing pizza wasn't quite so difficult.

The funny thing is, it took me three hours of trying stuff on this afternoon – with Sandie acting as my stylist – to come up with this particular outfit (the strangling polo, my best jeans, my least scuffed trainers) and now I was so uncomfortable that I'd have preferred to show up for my date with Keith Brownlow in my dressing gown and PJs. Although that *might* have attracted a few stares as I hovered outside La Porchetta Pizza waiting for him...

Waiting for Keith: that had been like a form of torture. Nerves were making me hyperventilate so much that by the time he came slouching along the road, I thought I might *faint* through lack of oxygen to my brain.

Having said that, the conversation we had in the pizza place didn't really *need* that many brain cells.

An example:

"I don't like olives," Keith mumbled, pinging yet another black olive off his pepperoni pizza with the tip of his fork. "Why do they put them on there?"

He had a little soggy pile of them at the side of his plate. Heaped together like that, they looked a bit like the rabbit poo I'd helped Tor clean out of Cilla the bunny's hutch this morning.

"I dunno," I shrugged. "Y'know, once, I asked for a pizza and it came with *anchovies* on it. They're disgusting. I mean, little fish on a pizza? That's *too* freaky..."

If Billy had been sitting across from me, that'd have got us prattling away, coming up with loads more disgusting toppings for pizzas. Whipped cream, boiled eggs, Brussels sprouts, jelly beans, mince, prunes, slugs (very like anchovies) ... we'd have had a ball. But I had Keith Brownlow for company, and all he did after I said that was point to another olive lurking under a slice of pepperoni and grumble, "Look! There's another one!"

Course, in the hour it took to have our pizza, we didn't *just* talk about Keith's hatred of olives; we covered stuff like Keith's favourite brand of trainers, Keith's favourite sports programme, Keith's amazing goal last Sunday and Keith's favourite type of chip (thick-cut, in case you were dying to know...). Do you see any kind of pattern emerging here? As I listened to him yakking on about how much memory his computer had, a lightbulb-type thought struck me – conversations should be like that game of Word Association or whatever it's called. You know, the one where someone says, "crisps", then the next person says "nuts", and the next says "Rowan" and so on. In other words, what each person says should link up to whatever the *last* person said, even if it's just loosely. And basically, that just wasn't happening with me and Keith. *I'd* try and start up something ("Hey, I went to the dress rehearsal for the school fashion show today – it was a total disaster!"), and then Keith would nod and change the subject ("Oh, yeah? Anyway, about this mad website I found…"). It was like we were having two totally separate conversations.

And of course, the *other* major hassle was no "Ahh" factor. By that I mean, when I looked at Keith, there was a bit of "Ooh" going on all right, as in, "Ooh, I can't quite believe I'm out on a date, with a *boy*!". But there was definitely no "Ahh", as in, "Ahh … he's *lovely*", or better still, "Ahh … *Alfie*."

I hated to say this, but maybe Billy was right. If you don't fancy someone, what's the point in going out with them? And I hated to say this even more, but *maybe* he was right about Keith Brownlow being a boring git too…

Precisely sixty-two minutes after we went in to La Porchetta (I was checking my watch, believe me), me and Keith split the bill (bang went my entire week's allowance), got our coats on (I managed to knock over a vase with a carnation in it with my sleeve), and started walking to the door.

I tell you, I felt terrible. I had a really bad belly-ache, as well as a thumping head. I knew what was causing the belly-ache – pizza and stress is *so* not a good combination. And as for the head-thumping, well, that was down to the fact that I knew a) me and Keith Brownlow were *also* not a good combination, and b) in two seconds flat I would be standing outside the restaurant, wondering how exactly to give Keith the brush-off, before *he* gave *me* the brush-off.

"So, um, Ally, I was thinking..." I heard Keith mutter just behind me as we got to the door.

But I didn't catch the rest of what he said, since my attention was slightly grabbed by spotting Chloe and her family being shown to a table, about five centimetres away from me. Her parents and kid brothers weren't looking my way, but Chloe certainly was – giving me, and then Keith, a very surprised *glare*.

"...so what do you reckon?" I suddenly tuned back into Keith's sentence. Pity I didn't know what had gone on in the middle of it.

"Huh?" I twisted round and blinked at him.

"About coming to watch me play football tomorrow afternoon. You fancy it?" he shrugged.

Out of the corner of my eye, I saw that Chloe was following her family, but still had her pinched white face turned in our direction, *straining* to listen in, I bet.

"Sure! Sure I'd *LOVE* to come and watch you play football tomorrow!" I heard myself lie *very* loudly.

Keith jumped a bit at that blast of enthusiasm, but there you go. It was a case of mission accomplished – I peeked fast and saw Chloe's cheeks flush pink with surprise. Ha! She didn't much like the fact that I was seeing someone, did she? Now it was *my* turn to have a little smirk, just like Chloe had smirked at me this afternoon from the stage.

Er, only *one* problem. There was nothing I fancied *less* than spending Sunday afternoon in the freezing cold watching boring Keith Brownlow boot a ball around a patch of grass...

Chapter 18

THE BRANCH IN THE BASEBALL CAP...

Time: Sunday afternoon.

Place: Football pitch at the Old Racecourse in Ally Pally park (watching Keith Brownlow and loads of other boys running around shouting in spectacularly short shorts).

Weather: Arctic cold with a light smattering of snow (expect to see penguins anytime soon).

Boredom levels: Rising as the temperature falls...

"Um, Ally..." Sandie muttered dubiously, bouncing slightly by my side as she struggled to keep her body temperature above freezing, even though she was dressed in something that looked more like a *duvet* than a coat.

"What?" I asked her, as I bent down to pat Rolf and Winslet.

(Winslet growled, so I gave up. Both dogs were sulking with me for putting their leads on, but it was their own fault for trying to join in with the football match. You should have *seen* the look Keith gave me when Rolf tried to eat the ball, and the referee positively *glowered* at me when I had to go into the goal and pull Winslet out after she ran in there and peed on the back of the net...)

"Look – over there!" Sandie nodded in the direction of a bunch of trees.

At first, I couldn't see anything. Then I spotted it – a low-down tree branch or something *moved*. Wait a minute; *was* it a branch? Or a passing penguin? Only one thing; I'd never known a branch or a penguin to wear a baseball cap...

"That's Billy, isn't it?" said Sandie, just as Rolf and Winslet's doggy radar kicked in and they began to bark a frenetic hello in the direction of the trees. They'd only seen Billy – and his demented poodle Precious – a couple of hours ago when we met up for our usual Sunday morning walk in the park, but my hairy hounds were acting like he was some long-lost relative.

"Shush!" I attempted to shut them up, as the referee shot me a look – but what could I do? I couldn't exactly *help* it if Rolf and Winslet were distracting the teams from their important business of running and shouting in their short shorts.

Course, the referee and the teams weren't the only ones to be distracted by the ear-splitting barking going on – the immediate effect it had on Billy was to make him leap behind a tree. (Pity the peak of his baseball cap was sticking out and giving him away.) Then he must have decided that hiding was a pretty naff idea, since me, Sandie and the dogs were all standing staring in his direction.

"What is he *doing* here?" I grumbled, as I watched him come out from behind the tree and stomp over the tangle of snow-covered grass and shrubbery towards us – with the most sheepy of sheepish grins on his face, it has to be said.

"Did you tell him you were coming to watch Keith this afternoon?" Sandie quizzed me.

"Well, yes – I mentioned *something* about it when I saw him this morning…"

Here's how it came about: Billy said, "Fancy going to see a movie this afternoon?"; I said, "No, I can't. I'm skint. And I'm busy"; Billy said, "Doing what?", and I tried to come up with a lie, since I didn't want to have some big downer discussion about Keith, but being pretty lousy at lying, I said straight out, "Keith's got a match on. I said I'd go and watch"; Billy didn't say anything – he was too busy snorting; I told him to stop snorting or I'd go home; Billy didn't stop snorting, so I went home. The end. Until he showed up right now…

"Hey! Fancy seeing you guys here!" Billy tried to joke, as he approached us.

"Yeah, and fancy seeing *you* here when I told you earlier this was where I was coming this afternoon!" I frowned at him.

"Oh, was it *here* you said the match was on? I, er, don't remember you mentioning that, Ally!"

Like me, Billy is lousy at lying.

"Billy Stevenson – your pants are *so* on fire…"

"She means you're fibbing," Sandie butted in, explaining what I meant when she really didn't have to. Billy knew all too well what I was getting at.

"It's just … well, I just thought I'd come down and…"

I set a killer death ray stare on Billy as he struggled to come up with a half-decent reason for spying on me.

"…maybe keep you company, s'all," he mumbled

feebly. "Thought I could maybe explain what was going on, since you know absolutely zilch about football."

I might know zilch about football, but there was one thing I knew for sure – you don't come and watch your sort-of-boyfriend play a game with your boy mate in tow.

"And how's it going to look to Keith if he sees you standing here with me?" I pointed out to Billy. "This is supposed to be a date, y'know!"

"Well, what's *she* doing here, then!" Billy stuck his finger in the direction of the walking duvet that contained Sandie.

"*Girl* mates are allowed to hang around on dates!" she snapped at him.

"Since when?" blustered Billy.

"Since for ever! It's just a rule. *Everyone* knows that!"

Sandie was enjoying this, I could tell. Normally, Billy is the one teasing *her* (which doesn't please my shy, easily flustered buddy one bit). Any chance she got to needle him in return, she jumped on it. But there was something I had to clear up with her here...

"But, Sandie, you *are* just keeping me company till the end of the match, right?" I reminded her of our agreement. I was very, *very* grateful to her for offering to hang around with me for a while, so I didn't look like a complete lemon, hovering here on my own (with mad dogs) by the edge of the pitch. But after Keith had finished his game and changed out of his short shorts and into something more sensible (i.e. something that would stop his legs getting frostbite), she was going to skedaddle and leave us to it. That was the deal. 'Cause after that, it was going to be just me and Keith ... and today, I decided, was going to be the last chance I was going to give this ... this *"relationship"* thing, or whatever it was that was supposed to be going on between us. It was just that if we had *one* more conversation that consisted of Keith Brownlow listing his highest scores on his favourite PlayStation games in descending order while I just nodded, then I was – eek! – going to *have* to chuck him*.

(*I had absolutely no idea how you were meant to do that, and lay in bed all last night feeling sick about it. I was beginning to wish I'd never gone out with him in the first place, then I'd never have had to worry about the chucking thing. Then again, maybe I'd fall madly in love with him today and that would be it – I wouldn't have to chuck him at all! Unless of course he decided he didn't like *me*, and gave *me* the elbow. Oh, God...)

"Course I'll go *then*!" Sandie interrupted my current bout of fretting.

Half of me didn't want her to go at all – half of me wanted to beg her to stay so I wasn't left alone with Keith Brownlow and his boring conversation. And then half of me wanted to leave right now with her and Billy and go and get a hot chocolate in the café by the duck pond. But another half of me (wow – that's a lot of halves, isn't it?) sort of wanted to go out with Keith, just to annoy my ex-friend Chloe Brennan...

"Well, since *she*'s staying, can't *I* stay till the end of the game, Ally?" Billy asked me appealingly.

"Billy – are you a girl?" Sandie quizzed him sternly.

"Not last time I looked…" he mumbled.

I almost smiled, but stopped myself just in time. I was annoyed at Billy for coming to spy on me, I had to remind myself.

"Well, if you're *not* a girl, then you can't hang around. It's the rule, remember?"

Billy pursed his lips in the direction of Sandie, as if he was trying very hard to hold in some sarky comment that was struggling to sneak out of his mouth.

"See you, then, Ally…" he mumbled instead, fiddling with the brim of his baseball cap as he turned forlornly away from us and started to stomp across the snowy grass.

I didn't know it was possible to walk sadly, but somehow Billy managed it. Rolf saw it too – that gloomy slouch and soulful shuffle – and began to howl. Now, I felt *really* muddled; I wasn't sure whether I was still angry enough to want to punch Billy, or felt so guilty that I wanted to shout to him to come back…

"He's putting it on," said Sandie, crossing her arms in front of her duvet-padded chest.

I wasn't so sure, till Billy suddenly turned round with a grin and called out, "Sorry? Did you say something, Ally? Did you beg me to stay?"

He sure got the message when me and Sandie started pelting him with snowballs…

"…and our manager says that the new kit is going to have blue socks and…"

I've got to chuck him.

"...the car I want when I pass my test is a Lotus, 'cause they're the coolest and the engine size is..."

I've got to chuck him.

"...and the thing about the StarTac mobile is that it's..."

I've got to chuck him.

"...so Ben says to me, 'Keith, I bet you a fiver you can't get to Level 6' and I says to Ben..."

Omigod, here's my house, here's my gate – I really am going to have to chuck him any second now.

Yep, Keith had walked me home after football and bored me more stupid than I thought it was humanly possible to do. I'd had better conversations with Tor's iguana; at least it tilted its head occasionally so that it looked like it was mildly interested in what I had to say – which was more than Keith Brownlow had managed. In fact, my favourite bits of the walk home had been when he took a slug of his can of Coke (which he didn't offer to me, by the way), 'cause at least it stopped him – for a few, fleeting, *blissful* seconds – from drivelling on about football/cars/mobile phones/computer games/mobile phones with computer games on them/computer games about football or cars.

"Well, this is me!" I muttered, coming to a stop by my gate.

(My heart was thundering so fast that I was sure Keith would be able to see my chest vibrating.)

"Yeah...?" Keith nodded, hoisting his Adidas sports bag further up on to his shoulder and taking another slug of Coke.

"Yeah."

(I was nodding too much – he'd think I'd suddenly developed a crippling disease of the nervous system.)

"Well…" he shrugged.

(Well, I was about to chuck him, but found that no words at all were coming out of my open mouth. I must have looked like a traumatized goldfish. I must have— *Oooooh! Ahhhhhh!*)

I didn't see *that* coming. And you kind of *want* to know your first kiss is about to happen, don't you? But it was sure one big surprise to me. One minute, I was doing the traumatized goldfish thing, and the next I had someone's mouth on mine, sliding around in a way I wasn't really sure if I liked.

Maybe I'm supposed to make my lips go softer, I panicked, feeling the warm wetness of Keith's Coke-flavoured lips. *Maybe I'm meant to move them about or something…*

I seriously didn't know what I was meant to be doing, and I couldn't for the life of me remember one single solitary tip about kissing in any of the magazines I'd read. But – *bleurgghhhh!* – surely one of the things you're *not* meant to do when you're kissing is *burp in a girl's mouth…*

"Um, sorry … Coke…" Keith broke away and blushed furiously, holding his can up like I couldn't have guessed the cause of that belch.

"Uh-huh…" I nodded, knowing my cheeks were a matching shade of red to his.

"Better go," I heard Keith say, before he disappeared

in a blur down our street. (He should go in for the school sprint team, as well as the football team.)

So ... I'd just had my first kiss. And instead of walking on air while rose petals rained from the sky, all I knew was that I felt slightly sick...

"Hey, Ally Pally!" Dad grinned at me as I slammed the front door shut and bolted for the stairs. "Where you going?"

"Got to brush my teeth!" I replied, ready to take the steps two at a time.

"Er, hold on a minute, there, Al! Haven't you forgotten something?"

Four steps up I stopped and gazed back down at my dad. He was standing in the hall, hands in his jeans' pocket, nodding down at a panting Winslet.

It took me a second (I was still in shock from the worst first kiss in the world) to figure out what was wrong.

Good grief: I was one dog short...

Chapter 19

MISSING: ONE DUMB DOG

"Rolfy! Here boy! Got something for you!" Rowan called out, while loudly tapping a fork on a can of Tesco doggy chunks she'd grabbed from the house.

Far away, there came the sound of barking, but not the right sort: it was only Winslet calling out for her best buddy, or getting excited at the sound of the Tesco doggy chunks...

Oh God.

I had *no* idea where I'd lost Rolf. I'd been so wound up about Keith "Burper" Brownlow all this afternoon that I hadn't given the dogs a second thought. Last time I consciously remembered noticing Rolf was when he was howling like an orphaned wolf-cub as Billy bumbled off. I'd let both the dogs off the lead around then as the match was almost finished.

"*Alleeeeee! Linnnnn! Rowaaannn!*" Dad's voice echoed across the grassy expanse of the lower part of the park. Not that you *could* see the grassy expanse, *or* any of the rest of the park – it was way too dark for that. All you could make out in the distance was the bobbing beams of two detached bicycle headlamps (being used by Dad and Tor as torches), a pair of luminous deely-boppers (Tor's – bought last Bonfire Night) and a circle of flashing red dots (not an alien space craft, but Winslet's Christmas collar).

"Maybe Dad's calling 'cause they've found him!" Rowan suggested hopefully.

"Nope, he'd have shouted that," Linn announced, letting the beam from her torch wander wildly as she pulled back the cuff of her coat sleeve and pushed the glow-in-the-dark button on her watch face. "It's half-five. Time to give up for the day – just like Dad suggested."

That had been the agreement when we started this – we'd split up into two search parties, with Dad, Tor and Winslet going one way, and me, Linn and Rowan going the other. We'd hunt for Rolf till we found him, or it got to 5.30 p.m. – whichever came first. And now it was late and cold and snowing and Rolf was out here somewhere, lost, and it was all my stupid fault.

"Tor's going to *hate* me!" I whined, waving my torch around frantically, desperate to see a dumb, drooling dog caught in the beam of it.

"He's not going to hate you," said Linn, in a sensible and practical voice (the sort Grandma tends to use when she spots that one of us is about to get hysterical over something or other). "He knows you didn't lose Rolf deliberately."

It didn't matter to me whether Tor thought it was deliberate or not – all I knew was that it was going to break my little brother's heart if that bundle of fur didn't show his hairy face soon.

"It's all my fault!" I whimpered, my own heart weighed down with guilt as we walked over towards Dad, Tor and Winslet.

"It's *not* your fault!" Rowan tried to soothe me, rubbing my back. "Well, OK, *technically*, it *is* your fault, but, well, none of us have been very nice to Rolf lately! We've all been getting really annoyed and grumpy with him!"

Rowan's words didn't exactly do much to comfort me, and neither did the back-rubbing she was doing – the fork she was holding was poking holes in my jacket.

"What *are* you on about, Ro?" Linn asked grouchily. "Are you saying that Rolf ran away from home because we were all getting 'grumpy' with him?!"

Great... I'd not only lost one of our prized pets – I'd also managed to come up with a new topic for my sisters to argue over.

"No sign, then?" Dad called out, before Rowan could answer and war could be declared between her and Linn.

"No," Linn replied, immediately going over and giving the Tor-sized outline with the deely-boppers a hug. "No sign. What now?"

"Well, there's nothing much more we can do for tonight," Dad sighed. "I'll put in a call to the police station, in case he gets picked up, then tomorrow I'll phone around some animal rescue centres."

"I'm sorry..." I mumbled in the direction of Tor.

(It was all I'd managed to say to him since I'd realized I'd lost Rolf.)

"Not to worry, Ally!" Dad answered in a deliberately chipper, cheery tone. "But we should hurry home now. I mean, someone could call tonight if they find him, couldn't they? His name and number are on his collar, right?"

"Um, right…" I gulped, my heart, my stomach, my entire set of *organs* sinking fast. "On his *normal* collar. But he's wearing his new Christmas one!"

My fault again – I'd put the new collars on the dogs and never thought for a second to transfer their tags. Oh, I deserved to be locked in a dungeon and forced to listen to Tweenies records for the rest of my life for this…

"Oh. Er, well, never mind," Dad said hastily. "We all have to remember that Rolf is a very smart dog, and he's probably found his way home already. Hey, Tor – what do you bet he'll be sitting on the doorstep, waiting to be let in when we get back?"

Tor said nothing. He might only have been seven, but he was wiser than our dad in many ways. And right now, I knew – without being psychic – what he was thinking: Rolf? *Smart?* Dad *had* to be joking…

LAYING (VERY) LOW...

It was Monday the 17th of December, it was the last week of school, and everything and everyone had officially gone Christmassy overnight.

God, or whoever, had arranged for a seriously thick blanket of snow to cover the ground. Miss Sylvester (aided by Linn and the rest of the organizing committee) was arm-twisting all and sundry into buying tickets for Wednesday's fashion show. In every class and every corridor at break, all you heard was people gossiping about what they were going to be wearing and who might (fat chance) ask them to dance at the Christmas party on Thursday.

Me? I was feeling about as Christmassy as a wet, windy day in March. No surprises that the no show of Rolf (still) was making me miserable. Yeah, so I wasn't alone there – Dad and Linn and Ro and especially Tor (who'd crawled into my bed last night after multiple night-mares) were just as blue and frantic with worry, but I had the added guilt factor built in, which made things a zillion times worse. Losing Rolf 'cause I was too busy thinking about Keith wasn't the only way I'd let down my family this weekend: I'd spectacularly failed to keep my promise to Grandma and hadn't spent one second rehearsing Tor's lines with him. (Mind you, after Sunday afternoon, I'd have understood if Tor had never wanted to talk to me again, never mind go through lines with the rotten sister who lost his dog.) Speaking of Tor, he was who I had to buy a Secret Santa present for. Good grief – what could I buy him that would make up for what I'd done? Maybe a dartboard with my face plastered over it? And if you want another reason for my non-Christmassy, bah-humbug mood, well, don't even *ask* about the ongoing silent treatment from Chloe and Co. Thank goodness for Sandie, that's all I can say…

"Duck!" squeaked my One True Friend, just as we left the exit door closest to the science block and headed for the side gate and home.

I wasn't entirely sure what Sandie was getting at – was there a small mallard strolling about in the schoolyard, lost and bemused on its way to the duck pond at Ally Pally? It wasn't *such* a weird idea; a whole flock of Canada geese settled down and roosted at the back of the school canteen one year when an outside pipe burst and turned the whole staff car park into a lake for two days.

"Quick!" Sandie squeaked, hauling me down behind a visitor's car by the arm of my coat.

OK, so either there was a really scary big duck out there, or by "Duck!" Sandie meant that we should lay low, pretty smartish.

"Um, what exactly are we hiding from?" I checked with her. The snow was so deep that, crouched down like this, the dampness was already seeping through my trousers and giving me an unpleasantly soggy bottom.

"Keith! He's just over there, with his mates!" Sandie explained, her saucer-sized blue eyes obviously much better than mine at spotting boys I'd rather avoid.

Oh, yes – since yesterday's mind-blowingly awful snog, I'd made a mature, adult decision about Keith Brownlow – i.e. I was going to avoid him at *all* costs and pretend we'd never gone out *ever*.

I know, I know, I *know*. That sounds pathetic, but at least Sandie understood.

"He *burped* in your *mouth*?" she'd cringed, when I phoned her last night (to ask her when she'd last seen Rolf, as well as tell her the trauma of the disgusting burp-snog).

"How far away is he?" I asked Sandie now, in a total head-spinning panic.

"Close. Well, close-*ish*," she shrugged, though it took a trained eye to spot that shrug through the mound of duvet-coat Sandie was wearing.

Now maybe Sandie is dependable when it comes to friendship, but I don't reckon much to her observational skills. This is the girl, after all, who convinced herself that there was a fearsome rabid fox prowling in her back garden, which turned out to be the new neighbour's elderly, half-blind ginger tom, looking for a new outdoor litter tray to make his own. And don't even get me *started* on the time she thought she'd had some life-threatening haemorrhage, when all she'd done was start her period. And *that*, in case you wanted an idea of how goofy Sandie can be, happened the day *after* the school nurse gave us a talk about starting your periods and what to expect. See what I mean? So excuse me if I sounded like I didn't trust Sandie's judgement, but I knew I had to check out Keith's whereabouts for myself.

"Oh, pants..." I muttered bleakly, as I peeked over the bonnet of the car and stared directly into Keith Brownlow's eyes.

Unluckily for me, I must have looked like a complete dork, crouched down and ogling at him like the saddo loser I was. *Luckily* for me, Keith didn't look like he wanted to acknowledge my existence any more than I wanted to acknowledge his, and it came as a supreme relief to see him look away and carry on chatting to his mates, as they kicked a football idly between them. (Not easy to do with 20 cm of snow on the ground...) It seemed like Keith was as mortified by the burp-snog as I was.

"Did you see him?" asked Sandie.

"Yep. And he saw me, I think," I gulped, as I slipped down beside her.

"Oh..."

"Exactly. But I think he's pretending he hasn't," I explained. "So, I think we've just got to get up, act like everything's normal, and make a hundred-kilometre-an-hour dash for the side gate. But acting casual, like."

"Whatever you say," Sandie shrugged, ready as ever to take my lead.

And so we slowly stood upright brushing the snow from our legs and bums, and clutching our schoolbags, tried to hurry – casual, like – towards the side gate.

Please let all his mates concentrate on the football, I prayed in my head, as we approached the steps that led down to the gate. If any of Keith's buddies began to call out to us, I think I (never mind Keith) might have died on the spot from sheer embarrassment…

"Ally! Hey, *ALLLEEEEEEE*!"

Billy. If there was ever a way of doing something wrong at exactly the wrong time, I knew I could trust Billy to do it. Right this second, all Keith Brownlow's mates would be looking this way and wondering what was going on. Maybe they'd start asking Keith what the deal was with us, and maybe Keith would tell the truth. Or maybe he'd bottle out and try and save face by making up some story about why I was too awful to go out with. Either way, Billy – sitting astride his mountain bike by the side gate in his Muswell School for Boys uniform and his out-of-school baseball cap – had made that all happen. Gee, thanks…

"What?" I barked at him. "What are you doing here? What do you want?"

"Got this!" he replied bashfully, hauling out a roll of coloured paper, a couple of rolls of Sellotape and a box of drawing pins from his rucksack.

"What is … oh!" I sighed, as he began to unfurl the sheets of paper and showed me (and Sandie) the "Missing" poster.

"After you phoned and told me what had happened last night, I decided to do this in IT today," Billy babbled. "I used that photo I took last year, when you and the dogs came round to ours and Rolf fell asleep in the deckchair. I got loads of copies done. I thought we could tape 'em round lamp-posts or pin them to trees or something…"

"Awww! *Cute!*" grinned Sandie, pointing to the poster Billy was continuing to unravel in front of us.

I felt some tears prickle in my eyes as I walked over and got a proper look. Apart from our phone number running along the bottom, it said, "Missing – Rolf!", above a picture of our not-very-long-lost dog, snoring happily on a stripy deckchair in Billy's garden. He'd been oblivious to the fact that Billy and I had perched a pair of sunglasses on his nose and draped a daisy chain around his neck as he snoozled. Oh, poor, missing Rolf! Where was he?

"D'you like it?" asked Billy nervously.

"Course I like it," I told my best boy buddy, going over and wrapping my arms round him for a hug.

And I didn't care who saw – Keith or any of his mates – *or* what they made of it. All that mattered was that I had a brilliant friend in Billy, bless him. That's when he wasn't annoying me stupid, of course...

Chapter 21

YET ANOTHER "SECRET" FRIEND

"It's not staying up!" Sandie moaned, as the poster of Rolf gently sagged away from the tree, flopping in front of her face with a faint rustle.

"That's because you can't *use* tape on the bark of trees – the tape's for wrapping 'em on to street lamps!" Billy explained to her for the fifty millionth time since we'd started on our "Missing" poster crusade. "Here – use these drawing pins!"

Poor Sandie; she was trying really hard to help, and I didn't want to hassle her, but glancing back down along the side of the street she'd been in charge of plastering with posters, I saw several more peeling themselves off trees as the tape came unstuck. I was going to have to go back down there now and re-fix them somehow, without Sandie getting upset at doing things wrong...

"Somebody somewhere is bound to have seen Rolf," Billy chattered away, as he taped another poster to a lamp-post, while Sandie struggled to untangle the tape that had just tangled her fingers together. "I bet you get a call soon, Al, now that these are going up all over the place!"

And they *were* going up all over the place – Grandma and Tor had gone out on poster patrol as soon as we got home with them, and Rowan had taken a load around the local shops (starting with Dad's, natch). Just before me, Billy and Sandie had headed out with our armfuls, Linn had arrived home and promised to go out and plaster up more with Alfie, when he turned up later. (Alfie, my knight in shining armour! And scruffy jeans, of course...)

"Somebody *better* phone with news about Rolf, or this is going to be the worst Christmas ever," I moped, feeling my thumb ache after pressing my thirty-zillionth drawing pin into tree-bark.

"Hey, isn't that your mate, Thingy Whatsername?"

I wasn't aware that I had a friend called "Thingy Whatsername", but I glanced in the direction that Billy was staring in, and saw a girl coming out of a shop, carrying a carton of milk. Even though the yellowish street light didn't cast much light, it was easy to recognize "Thingy", with her long thick dark hair and her accompanying three-year-old twin sisters skipping behind her, attached to her by neon kiddie reins. I hadn't even realized we'd got as far as her estate with our poster campaign, but here we were, just close by the entrance to her block of flats.

"It's Salma," I told Billy quietly, so as not to attract the attention of my no-longer good friend.

She'd stopped beside a tree and was frowning at the piece of paper flopping off it, as little Rosa and Julia collided into her legs, giggling.

"She's checking out a poster!" Sandie murmured, hiding herself slightly behind me, as if I was some anonymous, invisible entity, and not plain old Ally with a bundle of multicoloured posters in my arms. Which just at that moment were caught by a gust of wintry wind and rustled sharply, sending the top few spiralling into the frosty night air.

"Gotcha!" yelped Billy, making a grab for the getaway posters.

I don't know whether it was the rustle and flap of the paper or Billy's whooping that attracted Salma's attention, but all of a sudden she (and the twins) turned in our direction and peered hard at us through the twilight.

"Ally? Sandie?" she called out uncertainly. (Maybe she was just checking that us two and Billy weren't muggers disguised in school uniform or something.)

"Hi!" I waved, loosening my hold on the pile of posters and letting another couple flutter off into the night.

I half-expected her to go stomping off home after acknowledging that it was in fact us, but no – Salma came walking over with her sisters in tow, swinging her carton of milk nervously in one hand, as Billy sped by them to catch the latest runaway posters as they tumbled along the street.

"Ally! Omigod!" she called out, slapping her free hand against her chest. "I'm so sorry about Rolf! When did it happen?"

"Um, yesterday," I replied awkwardly, being slightly out of practice when it came to talking to Salma.

"Woof-woof!" said an identical twin who could have been Rosa, but equally could have been Julia.

"Nice doggy!" said ... the *other* one.

"Yesterday?" Salma gasped. "But you must be so worried! Why didn't you say anything at school today?"

"Because we haven't been talking for over a week?" I suggested, as Sandie nudged me from behind.

"Oh, that … yeah," said Salma, her shoulders sinking. "You know, I *hate* that we're not talking!"

At that, Sandie sidled forward, feeling braver.

"We hate it too," I told her, for Sandie's sake as well as my own. "It's all so stupid. That day at assembly, I didn't mean to sound like I wanted to be the winner of that competition. I only meant—"

"—that Chloe shouldn't have charged in there like she's the boss," Salma finished off, as her bouncing sisters yanked her bodily in different directions.

"Yeah, well something like that," I nodded, wondering why – if Salma understood the situation so well – she was still siding with Chloe.

"I'd really like to be friends again … if that's OK?" Salma asked apologetically.

"Oh, yes!" beamed Sandie.

"Uh, yeah, sure," I replied, a little more cautiously. "But what will you say to Chloe?"

"Well, that's the problem," Salma bit her lip. "The thing is … well, you know how Chloe likes you to choose sides… Well, I dunno, but maybe us three could be friends again – but in secret!"

Now where had I heard *that* before…?

Chapter 22

SHEEP, HAMSTERS AND THE LITTLE BABY JESUS

Unlike spectacularly average me, my sister Linn is a big hit with all the teachers at school. That's because she's supremely clever, dependable, reliable and sensible. (The fact that she's also pretty *and* pretty grumpy isn't relevant here.)

So who'd have thought she'd have been actively encouraging me to skive? Actually *holding* a fire door open and ushering me to sneak away, fast?

Of course it was all in a good cause. (But try explaining *that* to my scary Year Head Mrs Fisher if I'd been caught...)

Here's the deal: after Saturday's rotten dress rehearsal of the fashion show, it had been decided that there should be one more, last-ditch, panic-fuelled run-through, on Tuesday afternoon.

Everyone involved in the show (even saddo seat ushers like me) were excused from the last two lessons of the day, to go and do their bit in the main hall. Since my "bit" involved wafting my hand around in the general direction of currently empty seats, it seemed kind of pointless to be there. So I wasn't.

Instead of hovering uselessly around our school hall, I was now hovering uselessly around Tor's school hall, thanks to the fact that Grandma's cold had got a lot worse again (probably after trampling through snow putting up lost dog posters) and she couldn't go and help out at the Nativity play rehearsal like she'd promised. So – as arranged with Linn – I'd become her stand-in for the day.

"'Hello.' That's all you have to say here, Tor," a kindly voice said.

Out of the corner of my eye, I could see my little brother, dressed in a long brown robe thing with a tea towel tied around his head. He was standing stock-still and silent, even with his teacher Mrs Halston prompting him from the side of the stage.

Urgh... I should have done what I'd promised Grandma and gone over Tor's lines with him at the weekend: Keith or not, missing dog or not.

"It's so multicultural here at this school now," Mrs Goldman, the school's deputy headmistress, was busy telling me. "We're going to do this Nativity to celebrate Christmas, and then, we'll do something special for all the faiths on important religious days throughout the year, with all the children getting involved. It's really about letting them understand each other's—"

I know what Mrs Goldman was saying was very interesting and important and everything, and I was very flattered that she was talking to me like I was an adult (unlike most of the teachers at Palace Gates school), but there was something on my mind and I just couldn't help interrupting her.

"Um, Mrs Goldman – do you think Tor could be a sheep?"

Ten minutes after that request and I felt like I'd done something to redeem myself as a half-decent sister in Tor's eyes. Up on the tiny stage, a newly upgraded inn-keeper was proudly spouting Joseph's lines, word-perfect, while another little kid seemed delighted to have been given the role of the innkeeper, even though he was picking his nose. The girl playing Mary was singing "Twinkle, Twinkle, Little Star" to herself while dangling a doll by the ankle (the Little Baby Jesus) and a host of teeny-tiny angels (from the nursery class) were yawning or waving at the teachers or examining each other's wings at the foot of the stage. But best of all, there was Tor, in a cardboard tunic covered in white cotton wool balls, baaing softly and happily.

I may have lost his dog, but at least I made his dream of starring as a sheep come true...

Another ten minutes later, and the rehearsal was over, with a whole bunch of kids running wild, half in costume and half not, as their parents and minders turned up to collect them.

"What are you doing here, Ally?" Salma asked, appearing by my side with three wriggling little girls (the twins, plus her three-year-old niece Laurel) all trying to wriggle their way into their jackets but refusing to take their angel wings off.

"Skived off to help Tor," I shrugged. "What about you?"

"I offered to pick the monsters up today, to give my mum a break."

"You mean she *told* you to do it?" I grinned, spotting a

white lie a mile off. Salma loved all three kids and everything, but they did drive her insane.

"Yeah, well..." Salma laughed, knowing she'd been nabbed.

Ooh, this was nice – having a snigger over nothing in particular with my mate. I'd really missed that. It was just a pity it had to be in secret, same as Kellie, who was still going along with the blanking thing at school, except for the occasional wink she'd blink my way. What was it going to be like at the Christmas party on Thursday, with me and Sandie hovering on our own, instead of hanging out with the rest of the girls? I didn't even want to think about how rotten that would be...

"Ally?" said Mrs Halston, Tor's teacher, looming by my side with a strangely ecstatic-looking Tor. I knew he'd been pleased with his switch of character from Jesus's dad to barnyard animal, but had he got over Rolf already?

Well, not quite.

"Now are you *sure* you're going to be all right carrying this home today? It really is quite heavy, with all the food bowls and everything..."

Mrs Halston was suddenly handing me a large cage that contained a wheel and a mountain of straw in it. I hadn't the faintest idea what was going on.

"It's really terrific of your dad to agree to Tor having Max," Mrs Halston twittered on. "It was just such a difficult situation, what with things not working out with the nursery class. We really don't know what we'd have done with Max if your family hadn't offered to take him!"

"Naughty Max!"

"Bad Max!" babbled Salma's twin sisters, while her niece began to sob quietly at the sight of the cage.

"Is that the hamster that bites everyone?" asked Salma, who obviously knew more about this creature than I did, thanks to her small relatives.

"Um, yes, that's right, dear. Anyhow, it *is* all right with your dad, isn't it, Ally?" Mrs Halston frowned at me. "Tor said Mr Love was more than happy…"

I looked at Tor's pleading face, and then at the small pile of fur and fangs that had just popped up out of the straw.

"It's fine! It's absolutely fine!" I nodded enthusiastically, as I took the cage from her.

OK, so Tor had told a white lie, and now I had to too. But after losing Rolf, how could I let my brother down?

"Yeowww!" I yelped, as a small, razor-sharp set of teeth nipped at my fingers.

"You'll be needing these," said Mrs Halston, passing me a pair of thick, reinforced gardening gloves.

"Thank you, Ally!" Tor whispered, his eyes sparkling.

Aww – between the cotton wool sheep and the killer hamster, Tor had really started to cheer up. Now all we needed was for Santa to arrange for us to get our dog back, and our Christmas wouldn't be such a disaster after all…

Chapter 23

POTATOES TO THE RESCUE!

And so we had a new pet – Mad Max the ferocious, many-fanged hamster.

Luckily, Dad felt the same way as I did (i.e. anything to keep Tor happy at this difficult time), and didn't tell me or Tor off for the copious fibbing we'd done. Add to that the fact that Salma had explained that Mad Max had been destined to be put down if we hadn't come to his rescue (not a very merry Christmas for Max), which at least made my family feel like we'd done a very good deed indeed. Even if Mad Max didn't seem very appreciative and tried to bite everyone (including every curious sniffing pet) who came near him. Except Tor, of course – Max might throw himself hissing at the bars of his cage if any of the rest of us approached him, but all Tor had to do was coo a bit in hamster-speak and Max was practically rolling on his back waiting to get his tummy tickled.

The one person I didn't think would be too thrilled to meet Max (what with his bad reputation) or be swayed by the sob story of his narrowly avoided fate, was Grandma. So on Wednesday afternoon, I walked home from school, wondering what her reaction was going to be when I got in the house. Would Max be banished to the garden shed? Or would she cave in – against her better judgement – for Tor's sake?

Well, the answer was ... neither. Something had happened today; something awful that made Mad Max and his vicious habits pale into insignificance.

"What's going on?" I frowned, walking into the kitchen and seeing my entire family – including Dad – all seated around the kitchen table with Grandma.

From the uneasy expressions on their faces and the tears in Rowan's eyes, I knew they hadn't exactly been sitting around cracking jokes before I got in.

"Your gran had a bit of a scare today, Ally," Dad began to explain.

I'm ashamed to say I felt momentarily relieved – I'd been sure for a second there that they had bad news about Rolf, and I was guilty enough as it was about losing him. I really didn't need to hear that he'd been squashed by a runaway steamroller or something. But once that worry was out of my head, I switched to fretting over what was wrong with Grandma...

"Don't fuss, Martin!" Grandma suddenly told our dad off. "You'll just alarm the children, and it's not as though anyone got hurt or anything!"

"Except the mugger!" said Linn, with a hint of a proud smile on her face.

Good grief, what was going on here?

"Gran?" I squeaked, looking from her to my dad for an explanation I could get my head around.

"We've just come back from the police station, Ally,"

Dad began to tell me, holding out his hand to comfort me. "You see, what happened was—"

"Oh, you're being far too dramatic, Martin. Get me another cup of tea and I'll tell the girl myself."

That's our down-to-earth, practical gran for you – police, muggers; it was all a lot of stuff and nonsense about nothing.

"So what happened?" I asked, sitting down on the seat Dad had just left (and narrowly beating a cat that wasn't Colin to it).

"Well, I'd just been to the grocer's and then I went to the post office to collect my pension, and then I was about to pop in to the chemist for more cough mixture –"

Good grief – why do older people always want to load you down with heaps of irrelevant, mind-numbing details?

"– when this young man—"

"A mugger!" Tor piped up.

"—came at me and demanded I hand over my purse."

"Omigod! Did he *hurt* you?" I gasped, my blood immediately chilled to freezing point at the idea of someone actually *attacking* my wonderful gran.

"No – but *she* hurt *him*!" Rowan grinned, even though she was still dabbing her eyes.

"With potatoes!" Tor added gleefully.

OK, now I was seriously confused.

"As I was saying," Grandma continued, "I'd just been to the grocer's, and the next thing I knew I was swinging the carrier bags with the King Edwards in and ... and, well, I knocked him out."

"Cold!" giggled Tor.

Wow, my gran the hero! How cool was that?

I was still taking in this astounding information and getting all the gory details (the mugger was still unconscious when the police arrived to arrest him; the woman from the post office taped his wrists and ankles together with brown parcel tape, just in case he came to and tried to get away), when the phone rang, and Linn called out that it was for me.

"Hello?" I said warily, realizing I'd forgotten to ask Linn who it was.

"Ally! My mum just told me what happened to your gran! She was parking outside the chemist when your gran got mugged!"

It was Jen, babbling on like we'd never fallen out, all thanks to Grandma's adventure today.

"I can't believe it, Ally! How is she? Your gran, I mean. You must be so proud of her for being *so* brave!"

Maybe I was wrong, but I had a funny feeling that along with Kellie and Salma, Jen was about to join the "Let's Be Friends But Don't Tell Chloe" club...

Chapter 24

NOT SO ANGELIC...

"Would you like to sit here?"

"Hi – could you please move right along to the end of the row? Thanks!"

"There are three seats together over there, if you don't mind squeezing past everyone's knees!"

Oh, yes, I was a complete natural at this seat-usher business.

Except when I saw Alfie come into the school hall with Linn's other mate Nadia and went to pieces, of course. ("Woo– Woo– Woo–" I began babbling like a demented wood pigeon, "would you like to sit? Here? I mean only if you *want* to. Sit here, I– I– I– mean...")

It was also pretty awkward when I saw Chloe's parents and her little brothers – I had no idea if she'd told them we weren't speaking, but as soon as Mr Brennan boomed a cheery hello at me I knew Chloe had been keeping her business to herself, amazingly.

Next, I was chuffed to see something I hadn't set eyes on for a long time; all my old friends arriving together – Sandie, Jen, Kellie and Salma – who'd celebrated a Chloe-free evening by meeting at the Clocktower and going for a Coke and a catch-up at KFC before they'd come along. (Wish I'd been able to be there too.)

About a microsecond before the curtain went up, the place was full, and I'd have been able to scoot along and join my friends if it hadn't been for three latecomers in the shape of Dad, Grandma and Tor.

"Where have you been?" I whispered, as I led them to the only seats left at the back of the hall.

"Blame your gran!" Dad grinned. "We've been stopped a million times on the way here by people trying to shake the hand of our local hero!"

"Oh, Martin!" Grandma tsked, but she looked pretty pleased with herself, if you ask me. And quite right too.

"By the way," Dad whispered to me, as Tor charged ahead into the row of seats I'd led them to. "Don't mention dogs – we got a call before we left the house tonight from someone who'd found one, but it wasn't Rolf."

Yikes – now that he'd said that, I could see that Tor was looking a little mopey around the edges. Just as well he'd come to the show tonight; maybe watching out for Linn and Rowan on the stage would take his mind off you-know-who…

"Don't think much of the scenery," Jen frowned, as I sneaked into the last seat beside the girls. "Didn't Rowan have something to do with it?"

"No, not in the end," I whispered back, as the first models came stomping out on stage to the strains of Madonna's ancient hit, "Vogue".

The scenery wasn't much cop; it just consisted of a backdrop of white cloth with green and blue snowflake shapes projected on to it. It made me pine a little for what could have been, i.e. models tripping over confused huskies in blizzards of fake snow and dry ice, if Rowan had had her way.

"Look – it's your Linn!" Kellie squeaked excitedly, as my eldest sister came striding confidently on to the stage in knee-high black boots and a fitted, red, sheeny-shiny dress, her blondish hair scraped up into a chic little top-knot. She looked about two metres tall and totally amazing.

"Wow…" mumbled Salma, which is exactly what I was thinking, as Linn did this professional turny-spin thing and began strutting her stuff back the way she came.

For the second time today I was in awe of a member of my family, and this time it had nothing to do with potatoes.

After doing her modelling stuff, Linn must have been able to sit backstage and relax. Amazingly, after the disaster I'd witnessed at Saturday's rehearsal, the whole show seemed to go OK, with only the occasional person wobbling on their high heels or missing their cue and going off on the wrong side. The hour-long show was speeding by, and at last it was time to see what Rowan was going to spring on an unsuspecting world…

"Ladies and gentlemen, thank you for coming tonight and helping raise so much money for good causes," Miss Sylvester chattered down the microphone. "But before we finish this evening, we've got something very special for you: outfits made and modelled by pupils, on the theme of angels. Would you please put your hands together for the fashion designers of the future!"

And Chloe Brennan, who nicked the idea off her mates in the first place! I added in the privacy of my own mind.

Two rows in front of us, I could see Chloe's whole family were going bonkers at the prospect of their little girl's starring role. Pity they didn't realize their precious daughter was a cheat, *and* a complete bossy boots into the bargain.

Call me mean, but I didn't clap for Chloe when she led the troop of angels on stage. I saved my applause for everyone else, from the Year 7 girl who was so nervous that she practically *flew* her way on and off again in two seconds flat, to the wondrousness of Jason Bryant in his glittery Barbie outfit: silver-sprayed platform shoes, spangly skirt, wand and wings. Pity he had rugby player legs though. Still, it got him the biggest cheer of the night – until Rowan came on stage…

"Cool!" gasped all of my friends in unison at the sight of the gothic angel, in trailing layers of black lace (did those *really* used to be old white net curtains?). Pinned into Rowan's wildly backcombed hair was a pile of red roses (I'd wondered what had happened to that fake bunch that used to sit in the vase in the hall). But best of all were her huge black wings, made of even more black lace and edged in twinkling red sequins.

"That's amazing!" Sandie sighed, as Rowan began tossing spangles of gold glitter from her clenched hands as she walked, to the cheers and claps of the audience.

Quickly, I turned round to catch a glimpse of what Dad, Grandma and Tor were making of her outfit. I was pretty sure they liked it, from the way Tor was standing on his chair yelping while Grandma and Dad were madly joining in the applause.

They say things come in threes, and now Rowan was the third person in my family to make me feel choked up with pride today. (First Grandma, then Linn and now Ro.) If I wasn't careful, I was in danger of getting a little weepy around the edges with the emotion of it all...

Lucky for me, Chloe chose that exact moment to lighten the mood. With everyone still going wild over Rowan, Chloe began leading all the angels off stage. With a wave to the audience, she spun gracefully around and began walking towards the exit, giving everyone a spectacular view of her bum, thanks to the fact that her long, floaty dress was tucked into her bright pink knickers...

"Urghhhh!" I groaned, horrified at Chloe's gaff, being no stranger to making a fool of myself either.

Salma, Jen, Kellie and Sandie weren't so kind; along with everyone in the entire hall (with the exception of Chloe's family) they couldn't stop themselves erupting into giggles.

Speaking of Chloe's family, I just caught a glimpse of her mum and oldest brother spinning around and catching us, her so-called mates, in fits at her fate.

Which – I was sure – was *not* something Mrs Brennan was too thrilled to see. Why did I get the feeling that Chloe was going to hear about this...?

Chapter 25

CHLOE AND THE NON-STOP HAIR-TOSSING

It's funny how things turn around, isn't it?

Two weeks ago, I'd really been looking forward to the school's Christmas party – now I was about as excited as if I'd been diagnosed with rampant verrucas.

Of course, I was looking forward to it two weeks ago because at that point I hadn't a clue about Keith Brownlow fancying me; I had a happy home life which included a dog called Rolf; and a bunch of best friends I could always rely on.

Back in those carefree days, the only thing I had to worry about was what stupid, unimportant thing Rowan and Linn would find to argue over next...

"Why's she tossing her head around like that?" asked Jen, studying the strange movements Chloe was making on the dance floor.

"She's trying to show us what a great time she's having without us," said Salma, folding her arms across her chest.

And there's another example of how things can turn around: only a week ago, Chloe had made me and Sandie outcasts from our crew, but now she'd made *herself* an outcast by going off in a huff and having nothing to do with *any* of us. Mad, isn't it? I mean, it wasn't as if any of us had sneaked up behind her at the fashion show and deliberately stuffed her dress into her knickers for her – she'd managed to do that all by herself. But Chloe was obviously looking for someone to blame, as I found out last night when I was helping pile the seats up after the show had finished.

"I *know* you were all laughing at me, Ally Love!" she'd hissed, making me jump out of my skin and nearly drop a chair on my toe.

"But I—"

"My mum and my brother Paul saw you – all of you – so don't pretend you weren't!"

"Chloe, I—"

"Well, you and Salma and Jen and everyone can just carry on making fun of me if you want to," she snarled, "but just don't expect me to ever talk to any of you again!"

So here we were at the Christmas party, all of us together (without Chloe), all dressed up (Jen in those amazing black velvet trousers of Rachel's), having a lovely time. *Not...*

"She's going to get a headache if she keeps doing that," Kellie frowned, as Chloe continued to toss, toss, toss her red hair around as she bounded about in the middle of all the dancers.

"And I know for a fact that Chloe hates this record!" Salma pointed out. "What *is* she like?"

She was like someone who'd taken a big knock to her pride and was trying very hard not to let it show, I decided.

"Ally…" Sandie suddenly murmured. "I don't want to worry you, but Keith Brownlow and his mates are just over there!"

Sure enough – there was Keith Dullsville, ambling over and leaning on a wall not too far from us.

"Quick, cover me!" I squeaked, as my friends instantly shuffled all around me, acting like a human shield.

Why, oh, *why* had Mr Bashir decided to lump our two years together for this party? I'd done a great job all week of ignoring Keith (hiding around corners, ducking into empty classrooms, skulking in the loos until Sandie told me the coast was clear), but how on earth was I going to manage to avoid him here?

"He's just talking to his mates…" Kellie hissed, giving me a progress report. "He hasn't spotted you, Ally."

"Listen, if we all stick really close and start shuffling *that* way," Jen suggested, "we could make it to that pillar!"

"Jen, if we all stick together and start shuffling *that* way," I whispered to her in a panic, "everyone in this place is going to stop and stare at us for looking like loonies!"

"And this isn't an episode of *Scooby Doo* either – we can't all fit behind some stupid pillar, Jen!" Salma snorted at her.

"But I just thought—"

"Hold it! Check this out!" Sandie interrupted Jen, nodding over in the direction of Keith Brownlow and Co. "Look who's trying to butt in on their conversation!"

"What *is* she up to?" gasped Kellie, amazed as we all were at Chloe's stunning forwardness. Never in a million years would any of us have had the nerve to go up to a group of lads we hardly knew and just start talking to them.

But then *I* happened to know one of the lads quite well. Was that the reason why Chloe was now trying to do her hair-tossy thing in front of them? Was she trying to make me jealous? Had she fancied Keith Brownlow all along? Was that why she'd gone weird on me lately?

I didn't know the answer to all that for sure, but what I *did* know was that Chloe wasn't having much success with the boys at all...

"What do you think they're saying to her?" I wondered aloud, as I watched the lads start laughing and Chloe's face fall.

"Hold on!" whispered Salma, darting away from us and strolling purposefully towards Keith Brownlow and his mates.

My heart was in my mouth, trying to guess at what Salma was going to do. But all she did was keep on walking, straight past Chloe and the laughing lads, then in a circle through the packed dance floor to report back to us.

"They were teasing her about what happened at the show!" Salma blurted out. "I heard that Ben guy ask her to give them a flash of her knickers, since she gave everyone else a flash last night!"

"Serves her right," mumbled Jen.

But as I watched Chloe back off from the lads with her cheeks fiery red I couldn't help feeling strangely sorry for her...

Chapter 26

EMERGENCY! ANGEL NEEDED *NOW!*

I always thought the Angel Gabriel was supposed to be a boy, but not in Tor's school play he wasn't.

"Susan was the only one we could trust to say the lines," the nursery teacher Miss Joshi explained to me a few minutes ago, before she disappeared and left me alone with twelve distracted, bored, sleepy and confused three and four year olds. (Not my idea of fun, let me tell you.)

"*She* – hic! – stole my seat!" sobbed the inconsolable Angel Gabriel, pointing at another angel who had her tongue poking out.

"Look!" I tried smiling at the Angel Gabriel. "Here's *another* seat! Why don't you sit down there?"

"'Cause I wanted *that* seat!" whined Angel Gabriel (otherwise known as Susan Jackson) taking her wailing up a decibel or two.

You know, it's very hard to reason with an emotionally distraught four year old.

I didn't even know why I'd ended up helping out with the nursery class. I'd expected to be stapling kids into donkey costumes or woolly sheep suits or something since instead of sitting out there in the audience with the rest of my family, I was here behind the scenes at Tor's request.

"Please, Ally, please come help!" Tor had begged me last night, when he'd realized that I only had to go in for a half-day at school today. (The holidays start here – whoopee!) And since I was still officially the Loser of Rolf, I decided that it was only fair to do as he asked, instead of having fun and going into town with Sandie and Salma and everyone. (Ho hum...)

"What's going on here, then?" beamed Miss Joshi, bustling into the backstage room where all the nursery kids were waiting (im)patiently for the performance to begin.

"Um, *this* angel stole *that* angel's seat," I shouted, over the top of Susan Jackson's full-blown sobbing session.

"Oh, dear, dear, *dear*, Susan!" Miss Joshi said soothingly, while rolling her eyes at me. "By the way, thanks very much for helping out, Ally, it would have been mayhem without an extra pair of hands!"

Would have been mayhem? Angel Gabriel was having a fit, an angel at the back had fallen asleep across a desk, two more angels were busy pulling off their costumes and one was yelling, "Need to go to the toilet *now*!", and the whole show was about to start in exactly—

"Everybody quiet, please! It's begun!" whispered the deputy head Mrs Goldman, sticking her head around the door. "Angels – we'll need you in two minutes!"

"Do you hear that, Susan? We're going on in two minutes – so you need to calm down!" Miss Joshi tried to tell Angel Gabriel, who was having none of it.

"No! Not doin' it! No! Want my mummy – WAAAHHH!"

Urgh, I would have brought earplugs if I'd known how loud this was going to get...

"Need to go to the toilet *now*!"

"Well, you can't, Sa'eed, so just be quiet, please!" sighed Miss Joshi, trying to hug the Angel Gabriel as she began wriggling as well as screaming and yanked her angel wings off her back. "Don't do that, Susan! You have to go on in a minute and do your part in front of Mummy!"

"I wan' my MUMMY!" Susan screamed, chucking her wings at the angel who'd stolen her seat and catching her a glancing blow right on the side of the head.

"Woah! It's, um, OK!" I tried to calm down the latest sobbing angel.

"Need to go to the toilet *now*!"

"Sa'eed, I told you, you can't—"

"Susan?" said a woman's voice at the doorway.

"MUMMMEEEE!" yelled the Angel Gabriel, making a dash for her mother's knees.

"Need to go to the toilet *now*!"

"Not now, Sa'eed! Oh, Mrs Jackson – can you talk to Susan? We need to get her on stage any second now..."

"Sorry," Mrs Jackson shook her head, "when Susan gets into one of these moods there's no getting her out of it! She won't do it!"

"Need to go to the toilet *now*!"

"Sa'eed!"

"Miss Joshi – angels in one minute please!" Mrs Goldman stuck her head around the door as the sound of out-of-tune singing wafted in from out front.

"I better get her home..." mumbled Mrs Jackson, bundling the Angel Gabriel up in her arms.

"Whaaaaaaaah!"

Uh-oh – that wasn't the Angel Gabriel this time; it was the little kid Sa'eed, with a puddle of water fast appearing at his feet...

"Oh, no! Oh, Ally – help!"

I had absolutely no idea how exactly I could help Miss Joshi, apart from maybe finding the cleaners' cupboard and borrowing a mop. But obviously Miss Joshi had something else entirely in mind...

"Baaaa?"

I have to hand it to Tor – he may have been totally stumped to see his sister stomp on to the stage, leading a crocodile of thumb-sucking, hand-holding angels behind her, but at least he kept in character.

"And lo! There came a bright star in the sky!" I said quickly, as the hall erupted into titters.

Oh, yes – pure shame. I had taken on the role of the Angel Gabriel at two seconds' notice (thank goodness I only had three lines to say) but I didn't half feel ridiculous standing up there like some giant in my jeans and T-shirt with a pair of kiddie-sized white wings strapped to my back.

Gratefully, after my first line, I sat down at the side of the stage, glad to feel not quite so hideously gigantic.

But now that Joseph and Mary and the Innkeeper were stumbling through their lines, I got a real rush of happiness at being able to help out. As Tor – huddled in the straw by the crib – gave me a big goofy smile, I felt the small hand of a shy angel search out mine for a comforting squeeze, and by the time I had to say my next line, I couldn't stand up for more small, stage-struck angels cuddling into me.

As a teacher started plinky-plonking her way through the last Christmas carol of the show on the piano in the corner, I saw Tor's teacher Mrs Halston gesture at everyone to gather up on the stage, ready to take their bow.

"You were *great*," a sheep whispered by my side, while the other kids sang.

I nearly started blubbing right there and then, in front of all those kids and parents. I may have lost my brother's dog, but he still thought I was great.

And then it got worse – I looked away from Tor and out into the audience, and there was Dad and Grandma and my sisters, all beaming and laughing.

"Well done!" Dad mouthed at me, sticking his thumb in the air and getting me all choked again.

Weird, isn't it? Not so long ago I'd felt left out, knowing that Linn and Rowan would both be on stage at the fashion show, making Dad proud. And now here I was, making Dad proud of me too, in a funny, oversized angel sort of way...

Chapter 27

SANTA GETS IT *SO* WRONG

Cunning: that's us Love girls (and Grandma).

While Rowan went to put up more missing dog posters in further away areas, and while Grandma and Linn headed off to south London to scour Battersea Dogs' Home in search of a familiar hairy face, it was *my* job to distract Tor.

"What is it? What's wrong?" I frowned, as Tor came out from Santa's Grotto with tears spilling from his big Malteser brown eyes...

Good grief – what was Santa doing in there? Torturing small children? Whipping off his beard and telling them he was just an actor and that Santa didn't exist? This was the first day of the Christmas holidays – this was supposed to be a treat, for goodness' sake!

"Wanna go home, Ally..." Tor said forlornly, clutching a torn Christmas package under his arm.

The long line of parents and waiting kids outside Santa's Grotto in Wood Green shopping centre started shuffling uneasily at the sight of Tor sniffling. A couple of them even started to lead their protesting children away...

"Don't be silly, Tor! We've only just got here. Come on, tell me what happened!"

Tor sighed, then handed me the rustling paper bundle.

Slowly I unwrapped it, and then saw what the problem was: Tor's present from Santa couldn't have been more perfect, if we didn't have a lost dog to worry about, that is.

"It looks like him, doesn't it?" Tor snuffled, pointing at the goofy-faced, long-legged, sandy-coloured soft toy mutt.

"Not really," I lied, stuffing the toy hastily into my rucksack. "Anyway, what about the bookshop across the road? Why don't we go there next? I'm sure there's supposed to be something going on in the children's department today..."

Before Tor had time to say no, I quickly steered him across the concourse, hurried him down the escalator, and pushed him ahead of me into the bookshop.

"Look!" I said enthusiastically. "Told you something was going on!"

There sure was – tonnes of kids and parents were squashed into the back of the store, clapping away merrily.

"And let's all hear a big cheer for Spot to say thank you for coming to see us today!" the bookshop person was calling out.

Damn! We'd just missed whatever was going on. Everyone was cheering and waving at someone over there dressed in a ... oh, no.

"It's Spot the Dog!" whimpered Tor, at the sight of the bloke dressed in a brown and white spotted dog-suit waving his paw back at the crowds.

Nice one, Ally. Maybe I could take Tor to a dog show

next, or get *Lady and the Tramp* out on video to rub Tor's nose in it a little more…

"Now if any of you want to buy some of Spot the Dog's books, then we have plenty here— Oh! Oh, my goodness! Stop that *now*!"

Me and Tor scuttled to one side, to see what all the fuss was about, and soon "spotted" it (ha, ha).

"Ally…?" Tor frowned at me in a panic.

Wow, I was doing *such* a good job of cheering him up today, I *don't* think…

"So what happened then?" Rowan asked quietly, leaning back on the kitchen chair to make sure Tor was still out of earshot, happily playing with a growling Mad Max in the living room. (Who knew hamsters could growl?)

"There was this whole load of little boys – they hijacked Spot on the way to the Staff Only door and bundled him behind the Military History book section," I told her, flopping gratefully on a chair in front of the mug of coffee she'd just made me.

"Then what?" Ro asked, so distracted by my tales of our disastrous day out that she was finding it hard to concentrate on stringing thread through the spray-painted ping-pong balls she had spread out over the table (more DIY decorations).

"Well, *then* they tried to hold Spot down and unzip his costume," I explained. "Tor *really* didn't like that."

"Don't suppose the bloke dressed up as Spot did either!" Rowan snickered.

"Hellooooooo!" came a sudden shout at the door. We

couldn't make out anything after that since Winslet started barking like mad.

"Linn and Grandma!" Rowan widened her eyes at me, and we both dropped everything (ping-pong balls, cups of coffee) and rushed out into the hall along with Winslet.

"How was ... your shopping?" I white-lied myself into a conversation, as Tor bounded out of the living room with Fang-Face clutched in his hands.

"All right," Linn shrugged, aware that we were talking in code. "But we didn't get what we wanted, did we, Grandma?"

But neither of them had to say anything; the fact that they were empty-handed and dog-less showed that their venture to Battersea Dogs' Home had been in vain.

Oh Rolf! I sighed silently to myself. *Where are you, you big, stupid, hairy, adorable lump...?*

Chapter 28

ICE-COLD ICE AND HOT RIBENA...

Yesterday – what with the duff prezzie from Santa and the incident with Spot – had *not* been a great success when it came to cheering up Tor. Today could only get better, couldn't it?

"Billy! You're really annoying those people!" I hissed at him, as he and Tor came wobbling over to me at high speed.

"What people?" Billy panted, grabbing hold of my arm and using me as a braking device (nearly sending me splatting on my back, thank you very much).

"Those people over *there*!" I muttered, sticking a freezing-cold finger out at the disgruntled, snooty-looking family that Billy and Tor had barged into about a million times while they sped around the ice rink at high speed.

"Oh, them," Billy shrugged. "Bunch of bores. Aren't you supposed to have fun here?"

Well, Billy had a point, I supposed. Me and him had brought Tor into central London, to the outdoor Christmas ice rink in the courtyard of posh Somerset House to have exactly that – *fun*.

"Look, our time's up anyway," I shrugged, glancing at my watch and tentatively swooshing my way over to the exit. (I'm not too hot on skates, if you want to know the truth.)

"Awww!" Tor called out behind me.

"But that doesn't mean we have to go yet!" I added hurriedly. "We can still hang around and get a hot chocolate!"

Billy and Tor both cheered, and I decided to leave them to it, while I dumped my skates (phew) and went to do the café thing.

Fifteen minutes later, I was still stuck in the endless queue, waiting with a tray tucked under my arm. Normally, that might have made me kind of ratty, but today I didn't care; Tor was officially having fun, so that was fine by me. And I had to thank Billy for that – he'd whirled Tor around the ice for hours, long after I'd got tired out. Instead, I'd hung out at the side of the rink, watching them, catching my breath, listening to the fancy classical music that was drifting out from speakers and staring at the pretty lights draped all around the makeshift rink.

It was all so gorgeous; not just the lights and the music and the happy people dotted around the courtyard, sitting at the tables, but the fact that Billy and Tor were getting on so well, which they don't always. It's just that Tor is so notoriously quiet that it tends to freak Billy out, which is why my best boy mate usually refers to my little brother as "Spook-kid". But today, Billy had been amazing, which is just what Tor needed to cheer him up.

I couldn't thank Billy enough for doing what *I* couldn't do.

"Next, please?" said the girl behind the counter.

* * *

When I went back out with the tray laden with hot chocolates and crisps and set it down on the nearest empty table, I found myself slightly unnerved by *quite* how giggly Tor was. Not to mention Billy.

"Sorry I've been so long…"

"Pffffffffffffff!" snorted Billy, slapping his hand over his face.

Tor threw his head back and laughed like he'd just heard the funniest joke in the world. Even in the light-dappled darkness I could see that his cheeks were unusually pink.

"Um … what have you two been up to since I've been gone?" I frowned, wondering if Billy had been winding up the snooty family again while I'd been away.

"Nothing. Pffffffffff!" Billy cackled some more, glancing across at Tor, before the two of them descended into uncontrollable giggles.

"Tor?" I frowned some more.

"Heee, hee, hee! Ally – you want to know something?" Tor grinned mischievously at me.

"OK," I nodded.

Course I wanted to know something – I wanted to know what on earth was going on with these two…

"We've been stealing hot Ribena off all the tables!" Tor beamed.

I glanced at Billy, and saw him nod madly, dimples indented in his cheeks as he grinned dumbly at me.

"You've what…?" I repeated, raising my eyebrows as the truth sank in.

"Hot Ribena, Al!" Billy nodded madly. "Don't be mad – we've been nicking the plastic cups that everyone's left behind!"

Omigod...

That wasn't hot Ribena: I'd been stuck in the queue for the café for ever and spent part of that endless time letting my eyes drift over the menu. "Mulled wine": *that's* what was in all those left-behind plastic cups, not "hot Ribena".

Good grief. Billy hadn't just introduced my seven-year-old brother to the art of stealing (and stealing other people's leftover drink no less – blee!), but he'd also got him drunk too...!

Chapter 29

SING-A-LONG-A-CHRISTMAS-CAROL

"Ally, I don't think I can have any more..." Tor muttered forlornly, as he stared at the can of Lilt he was holding.

"Just a few gulps more, Tor," I muttered, lifting the can closer to his lips while I rattled the key in our front door.

Help: I'd never been drunk in my life so I had no idea if the Lilt (or Pepsi or Dr Pepper's) I'd made Tor drink all the way home would sober him up or not – all I knew was that I couldn't take him home in the giggly, pink-cheeked state I'd found him at Somerset House or Dad'd kill me. (By the way, I really, really *was* going to kill Billy, just as soon as I possibly could, the big berk...)

"Hey! Ally? Tor?" I heard Dad call through from the kitchen. "You're just in time! Come and see this!"

Quickly stuffing Tor behind me, I wandered into the kitchen, with an unnecessarily huge grin on my face. Luckily, Dad, Linn and Rowan were too busy poring over an edition of the local free paper to pay proper attention to me and my unnatural grin or Tor and his current fit of the giggles.

"Look!" Rowan pointed out, flipping to the front page.

Even upside down, I could recognize my own grandma...

"There's a story about her?" I gasped, scuttling over to the table for a better look.

"Yep," nodded Dad. "It's a whole piece about the mugging, and about what a heroine your gran was!"

"And it gets better than that," Linn laughed (a rare occurrence), flicking to an inside page before I could get a good look at Grandma's article. "See? That's a quote from me about the charity fashion show!"

"And there – that's me!" shrieked Rowan, pointing to a photo of her goth angel self before I could read Linn's quote.

"Wow! It's like the Love family weekly!" I smiled up at my dad and my sisters.

"And it gets better than that, Ally Pally!" Dad beamed, rustling to the next page, which featured a cute picture of some school's Nativity play ... starring one very over-grown angel. Eek! It was *me*! I didn't even know there'd been a photographer from the paper there!

"Listen!" Dad suddenly urged us, standing up straight. I may still have been getting over the shock of seeing practically our entire family splashed across the local press, but my heart still soared at the sound of the choir singing Christmas carols outside on our doorstep.

"Here!" said Dad, pulling a 50p out of his pocket. "It's not much, but go and give them this!"

Together me, Linn, Rowan and Tor rushed towards the front door, reverting to being about five years old and competing to see who could open the door first.

The chilly early evening air hit us slap on the cheeks as we gazed on the cheesily smiling carol singers chirruping out "God Rest Ye Merry Gentlemen".

Of the cheesy smilers, I recognized three faces straight away – Chloe's mum (yikes) and her two little brothers (double yikes), which meant Chloe couldn't be too far behind. And how she must have been hating every second of it – she moaned every year about her mother dragging her out carol singing with the church choir.

"There you go!" Rowan beamed, dropping the 50p into their "Save the Church Steeple!" fund or whatever was on their collecting tins.

"Thank you, girls! Thank you, Tor!" Mrs Brennan crooned our way. Ah, well, perhaps some seasonal good-will had made her forgive me for the sin of "laughing" at Chloe at the fashion show, even if I *hadn't* been.

As they said their thanks and began to move away, I noticed two things: Chloe's brother Paul giving me a withering look (unlike his mother, *he* obviously still bore a grudge against me) and there – lurking gloomily at the back – was Chloe herself.

As the others filed down our path, ready to hassle the people next door (uh-oh – the grumpy old Fitzpatricks; they weren't going to do too well there, *that* was for sure), Chloe shot me a quick look of desperation.

"Chlo?" I whispered fast, as she started dragging her feet after the rest of the carol singers. "You want to come in?"

I don't think pedigree racehorses could've moved quicker than Chloe, as soon as I said that. She was a blur as she turned and hurried into the warmth of our hall. It was only once she was in there and the front door slammed shut that she looked slightly panicked.

"You OK?" I asked her, as my sisters and Tor drifted away from us.

"Yeah ... you?" she answered awkwardly.

I bit my lip – it was now or never to sort things out with Chloe.

"I – I was really sorry for you. At the fashion show, I mean. With the knicker thing. I wasn't laughing, honest."

"Oh..." mumbled Chloe, rubbing her gloved hands together and staring at the floor. "Well, I'm sorry about ... about being mad at you."

"'Cause you thought I was laughing at you?" I checked with her.

"Um, no... 'cause you got a boyfriend before I did," she mumbled.

"What, Keith? You fancied *Keith*?"

"No! God, he's too boring for me. I kind of half-fancied his friend Ben, though, till he started teasing me really horribly at the Christmas party last night. But I wasn't even that fussed about him... I just... I just wanted a boyfriend. And I didn't want to be the last one out of us all to get one."

"Sandie hasn't had one," I shrugged. "*Or* Kellie."

"Yeah, but they'll probably get one before me, with *my* luck," she smiled wryly.

So *that's* what this had all been about? It *wasn't* that she fancied Keith – it was just that she'd wanted to be asked out before I was?

"You want a coffee?" I asked her, feeling like the ice needed to be broken just that little bit more. "I'll make it with milk – just how you like it!"

"OK," Chloe smiled, shrugging her coat off her shoulders and making herself comfortable.

Hurrah – me and Chloe had two weeks of weirdness to sort out but I suddenly, happily felt *sure* everything was going to be OK...

"Er, Ally..." Dad's voice suddenly interrupted us. "What exactly did you do to Tor this afternoon?"

"Hic!" hiccuped a woozily wavering Tor, swaying gently by Dad's side.

"Well," I grimaced, trying to think fast. "Have you ever heard of hot Ribena...?"

Chapter 30

INVASION OF THE SNOW ANGELS...

"Do you think we'll ever see him again?" asked Tor.

I hoped my brother was asking about the Santa Claus at Wood Green shopping centre, or the bloke dressed up as Spot the Dog in Ottakars, but I knew he meant Rolf.

"Of course!" I lied cheerily, feeling absolutely sure about nothing of the sort.

It was the afternoon of Christmas Eve and it was getting dusky. For the last hour or so, me, Tor and Winslet had been strolling through Ally Pally park (hard to do in knee-deep snow), pretending we were just out for some exercise but knowing in our heart of hearts that we were Rolf-hunting. Again.

"Maybe we should head home soon," I suggested, noticing the darkness starting to creep in at the edges of the sky.

"Not yet! Just a few minutes longer in case—"

"Hey, hi! Ally! Over heeerrre!"

Oh God, just what I needed – the boy who'd nearly got me into serious trouble with my dad (though luckily Dad was so cool and forgiving and thought the whole "hot Ribena" thing was a hoot) and his stupid yappy poodle.

"What are you doing?" Billy beamed, slithering down a bank of snowy slope to join us.

"Going home," I told him bluntly.

He couldn't get away with being all cheery, and trying to act all friendly like nothing had happened. I wanted *proper* grovelling from him, so that Tor got the message that the hot Ribena thing was no joke (even if Dad thought it was...).

"Aw, don't go home yet! We could have a laugh! Do you know how to make snow angels, Tor?"

Tor frowned silently at him, intrigued.

"Come on, Tor, we should go home. Winslet's belly's probably frozen solid," I said, scooping Winslet up and finding she weighed twice as much as normal thanks to the icy chunks of snow that had solidified around her miniature legs. It must be like us wearing a pair of wrought-iron wellies.

"Want to see the snow angels!" Tor announced, staring at Billy, as if he expected him to produce tiny, fat, fluttering fairy creatures from his pockets.

"Yeah? Well, here's what you do," said Billy, holding his arms out straight on either side and collapsing back-wards into the snow with a dull thud. "Then you move your arms backwards and forwards like ... this!"

He paddled them frantically in the snow, gouging out two wide swoops, as Winslet (still in my arms) and Precious (practically invisible against the white snow) barked insanely at his madness.

"Then you stand up carefully, and there you go! A snow angel!"

"Yeah, yeah," I said, pretending to yawn. I'd made plenty of snow angels in the past – with Billy when we were little – so it wasn't any big wow to see the angel shape he'd left behind in the snow.

"Wow!" gasped Tor, running over beside Billy's artwork and flipping himself back into the snow to make one of his own.

How weird... I couldn't believe I'd never shown Tor how to do this before.

"Come on, Ally!" Billy grinned, as Tor bounced up and then fell back down to make his second angel. "Your turn!"

"No way! I don't want to get colder than I already am!"

"Aw, go on, Ally! It's fun!" Tor called out, bouncing back up for a third time.

"Yeah – put the dog down, Ally, and have some fun. Or are you too old and boring now?"

Ooh, that got me mad. How could Billy say that, just because I was more sensible than him? (I mean, *Precious* is more sensible than Billy, but that's not saying much.)

I'd show him – *I* could have as much fun as he could...

Ten minutes later, the entire slope was covered in snow angels, some Billy-sized, some me-sized, some Tor-sized.

"Hey – we didn't do over there!" roared Billy, pointing to a smooth patch of snow close by, as Tor and I struggled out of the snow and tried to beat him to it, followed by Winslet and Precious going berserk.

And then the oddest thing happened... The dogs stopped dead, their jaws hanging open in mid-bark. Following their lead, Tor sat bolt upright, sniffing the air.

"What's up?" Billy turned and frowned, spooked by the sudden silence – which wasn't silence at all, thanks to that distant, happy sound of barking.

"Ally!" yelped Tor, his finger shooting out towards a thicket of trees halfway up the hill. "It's him!"

"What *is* that!" Billy almost squealed, seeing what could have been an alien spaceship tumbling towards us, its circle of red lights flashing in the growing dusk.

"Owwwwwoooooooooo!" Winslet tilted her head back and howled to the world the glad tidings that Rolf was back, back, back...!

"Can I introduce you to ... the best Christmas present ever?" I grinned, as Rolf battered into the back of my knees and practically sent me flying in his haste to run into the living room and lick our entire family to death.

"Rolf!"

"Baby!"

"Where did you find him?"

"Poo, he's smelly!"

"Why's he so fat if he's been lost?"

There were too many voices and comments and far too much barking going on to try and answer everyone properly, but one thing was for sure – Rolf hadn't been lacking food wherever he'd ended up because he had a belly on him to rival Santa's.

"Where could he have been, Dad?" asked Tor, settling himself down on the floor beside his beloved pooch.

"Don't know, Tor, but someone obviously took him in and took care of him," Dad shrugged, ruffling Tor's hairy ears. "But it looks like he missed us too much to stay where he was!"

"Hey, look!" said Rowan, pointing to a gap in Rolf's

doggy smile where a tooth used to be. "That's fallen out! Why would that happen?"

"Maybe it was rotten before, and we never noticed," Dad suggested.

"Maybe that's why Rolf was acting up and chewing everything that moved!" I chipped in.

"Well, well, well – the wanderer returns!" Grandma smiled from the living-room door, having come in with a giant brown-paper-wrapped box without us even hearing her.

"We found him in the park, Grandma! And he got fat!" Tor smiled happily.

"So I see... Got smellier too, I notice."

"So what's that?" asked Linn, nodding at the box Grandma was gingerly placing on the floor.

"It's from your mum. She sent it to my flat, probably because she thought there was more chance of me being around for the morning post than you lot," Grandma explained.

"Presents!" yelped Tor, scrambling over to the box to investigate.

"Ah, now, Tor ... let's put them all out under the tree for tomorrow," Dad told him gently.

"Well, there is *one* thing you can open now," Grandma smiled, handing a small parcel to Tor. "It's for all of you..."

Tor's eyes were wide – like ours – as he delicately untied the string bow of the parcel and pulled back the paper.

"Yeah! Mum made us an angel! We've got a new

angel!" he beamed, holding up a perfect, fat, black angel in a white tutu and wings, almost identical – apart from the odd bump and dimple here and there – to the one that Rolf ate.

"Give it here, then!" said Dad, standing up and going over to the tree. "Thank goodness Mum sent this! I thought we were going to have to give Mad Max a wand and stick him up here tomorrow!"

"*Dad!*" Tor snickered, passing the angel up to him.

"Isn't that weird?" Rowan blinked. "That Mum made us a new one, just when we needed it?"

"Well, you know what they say," said Grandma brusquely, "mums know best."

"Even when they're a zillion miles away from home?" I asked.

"Even then," Grandma nodded. "Now who's for a nice cup of tea?"

Staring at Dad, who was struggling to balance Mum's handiwork on our lopsided tree, I still couldn't quite get my head around the coincidence with the angel. But why strain my brain over spooky stuff I couldn't figure out?

All that mattered was that no one was arguing (for now), we had the perfect angel (for our imperfect tree) and Rolf was well and truly back home (as we could all smell).

Yep, tomorrow was all set to be a furry, merry Christmas indeed...

Lots of love (and a dog-food-scented lick from Rolf),
Ally :c]

PS For Tor's Secret Santa prezzie, I got him the *All You Need To Know About Earthworms* book – it was a BIG hit. For *my* Secret Santa, I got a signed, framed photo of Alfie (I wish). Nope, I got a pale blue karma bead bracelet (from Linn, I think). I look forward to wearing it … when I find out where exactly Winslet has hidden it.

PPS Me and Chloe and all the girls got together on Boxing Day and it was just like old times. We showed off our presents to each other, ate so much chocolate we felt sick, and sang rude words to Christmas carols. Perfect!

PPPS Rolf was much better behaved when he got back, although there *were* little reminders of his bad behaviour: the Christmas tree (and the living room) smelled of wee right up until we chucked it out in January...

brain full of plots, stupid stuff and cat hair

KMᶜC

the author

brain full of Pictures, football and cat hair

the illustrator

There's always something going on in

ALLY'S WORLD

1 **the PAST, the PRESENT AND the LOUD, LOUD GiRL**

My family's weird. I know everyone says that, but we are *definitely* weird. My eldest sister is 17 going on 70, my other sister is away with the fairies (literally – her room is a shrine to whoever invented fairy lights) and my little brother is a space cadet who's obsessed with Rolf Harris. Me? Somehow I ended up normal, but it's a struggle, let me tell you ... and I will tell you – soon as I get this vibrating three-legged cat off my head...

2 **DATES, dOUBLE dATES and BiG, BiG TROUBLE**

OK, so my dad's started ironing his jeans (yes, really) – something must be up. I mean, why would he slick back his hair to meet the plumber? It can only mean one thing – Dad is Seeing Someone. Like, a Woman Someone. And it can't be our mum, because she's still off travelling the world. There's only one thing for it – serious sisterly espionage. Hey, I know it's sneaky, but we have to uncover the awful (cringe-worthy) truth...

3) BUTTERFLIES, BULLIES and Bad, Bad HABITS

Rowan's been acting strange (well, OK, *more* strange than usual). One minute she's crying over who-knows-what, and the next she's tripping into the house with all this new stuff (which *has* to come from the shopping fairy, since I *know* she's got zero money). Then there's the graffiti at school: "Rowan Love is a muppet" (and I don't think it's meant in a friendly, Kermit-is-cool kind of way). Just *what* is going on with my sister?

4) FRIENDS, FREAK-OUTS a VERY SECRET SECRETS

OK, so I *did* have a best friend called Sandie, but I think she's been replaced by a Star-Trek type android. She still *looks* like Sandie, but since when did my *real* friend copy everything I do, and storm off in big huffs over nothing? I think the same thing's happened to Kyra's mum – the super-witch mum from hell Kyra's always moaning about actually seems super-nice. Have all my mates gone mad, or have I stumbled into Crouch End in a parallel universe…?!

5 BOYS, bROTHERS and JELLY-BELLY daNCiNG

Boys are weird things ... and just lately, the boys in my life have been acting even *more* weird. Take Billy, for example. He's been behaving like a total muppet (as the whole bra-on-head incident proves), and what's worse is I've been having unexplained *feelings* (like – eek! – lovey, jealous type feelings) for the big dweeb (*scary*). Not only that, but Tor's been acting strange too – something to do with boy mice, girl mice, and Mum. Confused? You're not the only one...

6 SiSTERS, SUPER-CREEPS and SLUSHY, GUSHY LOVE SONGS

So Linn isn't usually the most approachable elder sister (about as approachable as a grumpy wasp), but her "My family drives me mad!!" face has definitely been appearing more often lately. Maybe trespassing in her sacred room to answer her mobile wasn't one of my best ideas... Still, now we know that Linn's got a *boyfriend* – Q, lead singer in Chazza's band. Linn thinks he's super-cool, so why do me and Rowan get the distinct impression that he's actually a super-*creep*...?

7 PARTIES, PREDICAMENTS and UNDERCOVER PETS

So there I was, thinking that the last week of school was going to be mega-fun – I mean, there's the Fun Run, the end of term party ... OK, well *more* fun than usual. Could I have been more wrong? Urm, no. I mean, next-door's barbecue degenerates into a sausage fight, I nearly have to call the RSPCA on Kyra, the Fun Run is more of a No-fun Limp and, oh yes, how could I forget that disastrous game of Spin the Bottle...

8 TATTOOS, TELLTALES and TERRIBLE, TERRIBLE TWINS

Hurray! Summer holidays – nothing to do but laze around, hang out with my mates and have fun. Then Dad announces that his long-lost brother is coming to stay – cue Ricki Lake-style tearful reunion and everyone living happily ever after... Hmm, maybe not. Turns out that Uncle Joe comes complete with witchy wife and evil, pet-torturing twins. And evil girl twin seems determined to annoy all my friends, scare off my not-quite-boyfriend and generally ruin my life. *Fun?* If this is fun, I'm Kylie Minogue...

MATES, MYSTERIES AND PRETTY WEIRD WEIRDNESS

Spooky stuff's been happening lately. I mean, one little love spell and next thing I know me and my mates are running round Queen's Woods scared stupid. Then there are the mysteriously disappearing garden gnomes that have been reappearing in *very* odd places, and the weird noises and strangely misplaced knick-knacks (er, OK, that's not *that* odd in our disaster-zone of a house...). But here's the *strangest* thing: what exactly is going on between Billy and one of my best girl friends...?

DAISY, DAD AND THE HUGE, SMALL SURPRISE

Love is in the air! Billy and Sandie are getting a bit sick-makingly gooey, Grandma and Stanley are getting hitched, and Dad and Tor's new teacher are getting along just a little *too* well... As for me, Rowan and Linn, we're just getting scared – Grandma's told us our bridesmaid get-up has to be pastel-coloured. Pastel? *Blee!* But a looming fashion disaster isn't the main thing that's bothering me – I can't help feeling someone important's been forgotten in all this love stuff. Er, *Mum*, for example?

11 RAINBOWS, ROWAN AND TRUE, TRUE ROMANCE(?)

Alfie, Alfie, Alfie ... how deeply cool can one boy be? And not only is he drop-dead yum, but he's sweet and kind and has single-handedly turned Rowan into a local celeb! So why is Linn less than chuffed about this? And, um, why do I find myself taking the Grouch Queen's side for once? Well, my sisters might be having hissy fits at each other, but at least Mum and Dad are definitely back together, right? Er, wrong...

12 VISITORS, VANISHINGS AND VA-VA-VA VOOM

Well, *zut alors* ... as if by magic, a whole bunch of very cute French boys has just turned up in Crouch End. (OK, so it's *not* by magic, it's 'cause of a school exchange trip. Oh, and there're girls too.) Me and most of *mes amies* are desperate to get close enough to torture them with our terrible French. All *mes amies* except Jen, that is – who's just pulled a vanishing act. *Uh-oh...*

CRUSHES, CLIQUES and the COOL, SCHOOL TRIP

Yeah! Me and my mates are skiving school for a whole week! (Kind of...) We're all prepared for our geography field trip (apart from Kyra, who's dressed like she's going for a hike around TopShop). Only downer is, before we even get on the coach Sandie's pining miserably for Billy. But who'd have thought she'd recover so quickly...? Must be those super new *friends* she's made for us – er, make that super new *enemies*...

HASSLES, HEART-PINGS! and SAD, HAPPY ENDINGS...

Well, knock me down with a feather – just not one with superglue on (don't ask). The weirdness going on in my world means my head's even twistier than normal. First Sandie's parents break some big news, then Linn makes a scary announcement, and to top it all there's the, er, *heated* incident with Rowan and her Johnny Depp shrine. Nothing else could possibly surprise me ... not even if I opened the front door and found that I had a *boyfriend* on the doorstep... (Fat chance!)

for more gossip check out
www.karenmccombie.com

Welcome to a whole new world...

✩ STELLa etc. ✩

**The sunshiney, seasidey, gorgeous
new series from Karen McCombie**

① Frankie, Peaches & Me

Stella can't believe her luck. Seb – the boy she's
liked for for ever – told her he liked her too. At her
leaving party. (Talk about bad timing...) Yep, as of
today, her family's swapped life in London for a
sleepy seaside resort where the biggest thrill is a
psycho seagull. But how is shy-girl Stella going fit
into this freaky little town, specially without her
best friend Frankie? And what's with the suspicious
silence from all her other mates back in London?
Then – in a waft of peaches and cream
– a mysterious furry someone wanders
into Stella's life, and things instantly
start to get interesting...

2 sweet-Talking TJ

Stella's getting used to her new life in the sleepy seaside town of Portbay, but it's still a no-friend-zone (unless you count friends of the weird, furry, catty kind). So when she spots a scruffy, cute, friendly-looking boy on the beach Stella hopes he might be a potential new mate – him *and* his barking mad dog, Bob. But it seems TJ already has some dodgy mates of his own… Stella's confused. Why is sweet, goofball TJ hanging round with a bunch of total meatheads…?

3 meet the Real World, Rachel

Stella's got a new best mate (the small but cute TJ), and things in Portbay are now much more fun (like the hoax they're planning with the camera and the, er, fairies). The only hassle is Rachel and her gang, who still manage to make Stella feel like she doesn't fit in… But then all this weird stuff happens to Rachel, and her so-called friends start avoiding her. Has she been taken over by aliens, like TJ thinks? (Duh…) And should Stella come to Rachel's rescue, or is that possibly the worst idea she's ever had…?

And coming soon:
TRULY, MaDLY MeGaN